A neckerchief was t[...]
blue eyes peered up[...]
hair, sharp with de[...]
Casey Summerville—shook her head and fought against
her stays as well as the gag, groaning.

Longarm leaned his rifle against the bed and dug into
his pants pocket for his barlow knife. The girl grunted
and groaned, straining with more vigor, pleading with
her eyes. She seemed to want desperately to speak. Longarm left his knife in his pocket and pulled the gag down
onto her chin.

She lifted her head and, staring over his shoulder at
something behind him, screamed, *"Look out!"*

Longarm wheeled, instantly grabbing his .44. A man
behind him was holding a rifle shoulder high, butt forward, the man's dark eyes wide with cunning. He gritted
his teeth in a savage snarl as he thrust the rifle toward
Longarm's head.

The lawman jerked to one side just in time. The steel
butt plate grazed his left cheek a quarter second before
he rammed his double-action Colt into the man's gut and
triggered it three times.

→ TABOR EVANS ←

LONGARM

AND THE ARAPAHO HELLCATS

J

JOVE BOOKS, NEW YORK

THE BERKLEY PUBLISHING GROUP
Published by the Penguin Group
Penguin Group (USA)
375 Hudson Street, New York, New York 10014, USA

USA | Canada | UK | Ireland | Australia | New Zealand | India | South Africa | China

Penguin Books Ltd., Registered Offices: 80 Strand, London WC2R 0RL, England
For more information about the Penguin Group, visit penguin.com.

LONGARM AND THE ARAPAHO HELLCATS

A Jove Book / published by arrangement with the author·

Jove Books are published by The Berkley Publishing Group.
JOVE® is a registered trademark of Penguin Group (USA).
The "J" design is a trademark of Penguin Group (USA).

For information, address: The Berkley Publishing Group,
a division of Penguin Group (USA),
375 Hudson Street, New York, New York 10014.

ISBN: 978-0-515-15378-1

PUBLISHING HISTORY
Jove mass-market edition / October 2013

PRINTED IN THE UNITED STATES OF AMERICA

10 9 8 7 6 5 4 3 2 1

Cover illustration by Milo Sinovcic.

ALWAYS LEARNING   **PEARSON**

Chapter 1

"Is it hot in here, or is it just me?" asked Cynthia Larimer.

The deputy U.S. marshal known far and wide by friend and foe as Longarm couldn't resist. "It's just you."

"No, I'm hot as well, dear," said Cynthia's aunt, Mrs. Beatrice Schimpelfinnig, who sat to Cynthia's left in the Union Pacific coach car. "Maybe you could open a window, though the burning cinders from the locomotive are liable to set us all on fire!"

Cynthia and her aunt were facing Longarm, who sat directly across from the beautiful, stygian-haired Miss Larimer, bearer of the sexiest pair of cobalt-blue eyes and the richest ruby-red lips that the legendary lawman had ever known up close as well as down and dirty.

"I'll do it, Mrs. Schimpelfinnig," Longarm said, dutifully rising from his fair-to-middlingly comfortable, plush-covered seat. As he turned to the window, he felt Cynthia press one of her knees against his left leg.

The girl's flesh burned like the sun through a window in the middle of a summer heat wave.

Longarm glanced down at her, sitting directly in front of him, facing him. She was staring up at him with a schoolgirl's innocence. She wore a dark tan straw hat bedecked with a modest trim of fake pink flowers. Her silky black hair, gathered in a thick ponytail, curved down over her left shoulder to curl up against her full, round bosom pushing out her puce-colored, lace-edged, gold-buttoned traveling dress.

The lie was given to the innocence of the lovely girl's gaze when she very slowly tucked her lower lip under her upper lip, poked the tip of her tongue out from between them, and ran it very slowly back and forth against the inside of the upper one.

At the same time, she pressed her knee a little harder against Longarm's leg. She let her gaze flick down past his belly to his crotch, knowing, of course, the effect her leg and her lips and her eyes were having on him, and enjoying every second of it.

"Excuse me," Longarm said, glancing down at their touching legs and then smiling sheepishly at Mrs. Schimpelfinnig, who was frowning reprovingly down at the touching limbs, as well. "Tight confines, here, don't ya know," he said to Cynthia's plump, doting chaperone. He gave the middle-aged woman another witless grin, feigning innocence, and then turned his attention to the soot- and smoke-streaked window.

Longarm opened the window to the warm but fresh summer air rushing past the coach car, bearing occasional feathers of coal smoke kicked out of the locomotive's giant, diamond-shaped stack.

"Oh, that's too much!" Mrs. Schimpelfinnig declared, leaning back from the window as though a mountain lion had just poked its snarling head in the window. "Please, open it just a little, Deputy Long! You're going to set us all on fire!"

Cynthia's aunt brushed at the cinders that the portly, immaculately attired and coifed woman imagined had blown in on a few small snakes of coal smoke. She brushed her white-gloved hands at Cynthia's dress, as well, and Longarm couldn't help imagining his own hands doing the same.

And going even farther, of course. Working on those gold buttons until he had her dress open and pulled down to her waist, exposing those full, round, pink-tipped . . .

The federal lawman shook his head to rid his mind of the torturous thoughts as he pulled the window down to within two inches of the varnished wooden sill that was a maze of knife-carved initials. He noticed in passing that there was also one rather deft line etching of a man bending a bosomy woman over a rain barrel.

That didn't help ease the storm of nasty thoughts raining down on Longarm's incorrigible mind.

He glanced solicitously at Aunt Beatrice. "How's that, Mrs. Schimpelfinnig?" For his own selfish, lascivious reasons, he wanted nothing more than to not ruffle the woman's feathers. Only if Mrs. Schimpelfinnig let her guard down was Longarm ever going to get Cynthia off alone.

"That'll do, Deputy, that'll do," Aunt Beatrice said, waving an impatient hand in front of her face.

Longarm sat down and glanced at Cynthia. The

beauty was now biting down on her lower lip as she stared out the window and tried not to laugh at his obvious discomfort. She knew from experience all that was on his mind. For Longarm's part, he knew from his own experience what was on her mind, for he had learned since falling under the girl's spell at a Christmas party at the Larimers' mansion two years ago that she was no less robust in her desires than he was in his.

He'd been able to tell from the look in her eye and in the pressure of her knee against his leg that she was as eager to be alone with him as he was to be alone with her . . . and to roll that tailor-made dress up around her belly, to pull her under frillies down around her knees, and to go to work on the scrumptious vixen from behind.

The twenty-three-year-old beauty was, of course, the niece of Denver's founding father, General William Larimer and his portly, pale, but stately wife known to all who knew her as "Aunt May." Cynthia was on her way to participate in the wedding of a dear childhood friend who was about to marry a dashing young sheriff in the small, eastern Wyoming Territory town of Arapaho.

Since respectable young ladies not yet married were required to travel in the company of a chaperone, Cynthia had solicited the accompaniment of Aunt Beatrice, who often shadowed the precocious, adventurous young heiress on her travels across North America as well as abroad.

It was a good thing that she did, too. Who knew what trouble a girl with Cynthia's hot blood and wild heart would get into? Longarm, of course, *did* know. And he'd like to be reminded—the sooner the better.

That's why this was one time that he wished that Aunt Beatrice had stayed back in her stately Sherman Avenue digs in Denver, just down the road from the Larimers' own sprawling mansion. Longarm, too, was headed to the wedding at Arapaho, for as chance would have it, he'd been good pals for a long time with the dashing young, soon-to-be-married-sheriff's father, Thrum McIntyre, who'd been sheriff before turning the job over to his son, Ryan.

Since Longarm and Cynthia were headed to the same place for the same reason, it was only natural that General Larimer had asked Longarm to stick close to Cynthia and sort of act as the girl's unofficial bodyguard. Of course, the General had no idea just how closely the deputy U.S. marshal had been "guarding" the girl's body.

Longarm had no problem with doing so now at the General's behest. He just hoped he'd get to see as much of it as he had multiple times in the past, though if the vigilant Mrs. Schimpelfinnig continued to watch over her niece's honor like a hawk over its freshly hatched young, he doubted he'd get anymore than a flutter of the girl's smoky blue eyes and an occasional, furtive press of her knee.

Longarm was beginning to wonder if the cranky old bat had some inkling of the true nature of Longarm's and Cynthia's relationship. More than once since their train had left Denver's Union Station, he had caught Aunt Beatrice giving him the evil eye out one side of her fleshy face.

"I'm still a little warm," Cynthia said, waving a folded newspaper in front of her face. "I think I might step out onto the vestibule to get a little air, Aunt Beatrice." The raven-haired beauty arched innocent brows at her bodyguard. "Care to join me, Marshal? I'd imagine you'd like a cigar."

Before Longarm could answer, Aunt Beatrice said, "Those cigars are bad for a man's constitution. Besides, he'll just come back smelling like a saloon. I'll join you, dear. Deputy Long can wait here and make sure no one takes our seats. It took me long enough to find one that wasn't so badly soiled. Good Lord, what do these commoners do—transport their livestock in cars meant for *people*?"

Mrs. Schimpelfinnig had heaved her bulky frame, swathed in several yards of summer-weight gingham and capped by a plumed picture hat the size of a serving tray up from her seat, and stood holding on to the luggage rack above her head while catching her breath.

"Oh, never mind, Aunt Beatrice," Cynthia said. "It just occurred to me how windy it is out there. We'll both likely lose our hats and muss our hair. I'm fine right here. I might just doze until we reach Cheyenne, in fact."

"Oh," Aunt Beatrice said, glancing furtively and with an unmistakable look of shrewdness at Longarm, "that sounds nice, dear. I could do with a nap myself. We're so lucky to have the good marshal along so that we can feel safe enough to sleep amongst so many"—she craned her neck to look around the car—"unwashed souls. Why, to me they all look like train robbers."

Longarm felt crestfallen, but he managed to smile in spite of himself. "Well, now you got me thinkin' about a cigar, Miss Cynthia. If you and Mrs. Schimpelfinnig will excuse me, I do believe I'll head on out to the vestibule and indulge in one. Don't worry, ma'am, I'll make sure I smoke downwind so I won't come back smelling like a saloon."

"I would appreciate that, Deputy."

Longarm winked at the old bat and pinched his hat brim at Cynthia, holding her gaze for a beat, silently expressing his desire to throw her dear aunt off the train and into a deep gully where her stout corpse would feed the wildcats for days.

He rose, shuffled out into the center aisle, and moseyed out the coach's rear door to the vestibule, muttering under his breath, "Cranky old bat."

On the platform at the end of the car, the car itself shielded enough of the wind that Longarm had no trouble lighting one of his prized three-for-a-nickel cheroots. He didn't necessarily prize the stogies for their taste but for their price. A federal badge toter wasn't paid much more than a barman—he knew some Denver barmen who made more than he did, in fact—so he had to consider such things as money.

One thing he did not skimp on, however, was the quality of his whiskey. Longarm preferred Tom Moore Maryland Rye to any other tangleleg he'd ever sampled. It was a small, leather-covered tin flask of the precious liquid that, after he had the cheroot drawing to his satisfaction, he slipped from an inside pocket of his tobacco-brown frock coat that matched the brown of his skintight twill trousers and low-heeled, mule-eared cavalry boots.

"Be careful, old son—you don't want to return to the coach smellin' like a saloon," he mockingly remonstrated himself with a wry snort as he blew smoke out his nostrils and removed the cap from the flask.

Leaning back against the coach car's rear wall, his string tie buffeting in the breeze blowing past the gap on either side of him, he lifted the flask to his lips and took a liberal pull. He swallowed, grinned. He enjoyed the rosy glow the busthead instantly visited upon him so much that he took one more liberal pull before capping the flask and returning it to its pocket and following up the pleasant burn of the rye with another deep draw from the cheap cheroot.

He'd just turned to enjoy the view of the Front Range of the Rocky Mountains sliding past in the west, beyond the blond, gently rising prairie, when the train began to slow. He turned to gaze north along the tracks and saw a large wooden water tank propped on stilts. It stood just beyond what Longarm recognized as the Sandy Wash depot building, just east of the cavalry post, Camp Collins, where they'd be stopping for water soon.

It was a little jerkwater stop out in the middle of nowhere between Denver and Cheyenne. Longarm had stopped here countless times before on his way to and from assignments that had taken him north to Wyoming, Montana, or to the Dakota Territory, and he usually welcomed the chance to stretch his legs and palaver with the depot agent and the old half-breed who tended the place and acted as courier.

But today he did not welcome the delay. It looked as though the trip to and from the little town of Arapaho was going to be a tedious one indeed, and he'd just as soon get on with it.

Probably the only enjoyment he was going to get was when he met his old pard, retired sheriff Thrum McIntyre, and saw Thrum's oldest boy get hitched to one of Cynthia's friends. Longarm had never met Thrum's future daughter-in-law, but he had a feeling that since she was friends with Cynthia, she was most likely beautiful as well as precocious, just as Cynthia herself was.

A nice combination.

Seeing Thrum and watching Thrum's boy get married would under normal circumstances be worth the trip to Arapaho in and of itself. But having the intoxicating, ravishing Cynthia within arm's reach while he made the trip was no ordinary circumstance, though so far it had certainly been a frustrating one.

Thanks to eagle-eyed Aunt Beatrice.

When the train stopped, many of the passengers from the three coach cars left their respective cars to stretch and to breathe some fresh air. Longarm was about to disembark himself for a frustration-relieving stroll when, taking a deep drag off his cheroot as he leaned against the vestibule, someone poked a wet finger in his ear.

A soft, low, sexy female voice said into the opposite ear, "She's asleep, Custis, and I don't know about you, but I'm more than just a little bit randy. What do you think we should do about that?"

Chapter 2

Longarm turned to the girl staring up at him, her full lips quirked in a lascivious grin.

Longarm had to fight to keep from putting his hands on her. All over her. "I'd like to tell you what I'd like to do about that, young lady."

"Why don't you show me?"

Longarm frowned, incredulous.

"Like I said, she's sound asleep."

"What if she wakes?"

Cynthia shook her head. "She won't wake for a half hour, at least. I've traveled with dear Aunt Beatrice enough to know that when she starts snoring, she's out like a lamp."

Longarm turned to look through the glass pane in the top of the coach's rear door. The glass was badly smudged and it reflected the brassy high-country sunlight, but Longarm could still see Mrs. Schimpelfinnig— the only one left in the car after all the other passengers had gotten off to stretch—sitting in her green plush seat, head tipped back against her seat, lower jaw hanging, mouth wide open.

Longarm thought he could even hear her raucous snores through the glass. His heart skipped eagerly, quickened. He swung around to see Cynthia smiling up at him again. She arched a brow.

"This is going to have to be quick and very, very sneaky." Cynthia, who loved stealing quick pokes in the most trying of circumstances, let out a thrilled giggle. "And oh so naughty!"

Once, Cynthia had given Longarm a blowjob in her uncle's office chair at the Larimer residence during a Christmas ball. Her uncle, the General, and Chief Marshal Billy Vail had even been in the office at the time, though they hadn't seen her with Longarm's cock in her mouth beneath the desk. Longarm had had one hell of a time trying to converse with the two men while the General's niece sucked and tongued the head of his staff as though it were a lollipop.

That rendezvous had almost killed him. But he was sure that each of his unions with Cynthia had put such a strain on his heart that the gorgeous little black-haired, blue-eyed lass had cost him at least a couple of precious years.

He thought she was worth every lost minute.

Longarm glanced into the car once more, took Cynthia's arm, and said, "Right this way, my lovely."

He walked over to the top of the vestibule steps and looked around. All three of the coach cars were up train from him and Cynthia, so most of the passengers were up train, as well.

While the locomotive's boiler was taking on water, the men were smoking and kicking around beside the tracks, or gathered in clumps, smoking and talking, while the ladies also formed groups to watch their children running around the cinder-paved railroad bed and the wooden platform surrounding the little depot shed. One tyke was trying to climb one of the telegraph poles and being met with a crisp scolding from a woman wearing a red-and-green-checked dress and matching bonnet and holding a fussy baby in her arms.

The only folks down train from Longarm were a couple of brakemen in striped overalls standing around near the caboose, both men laughing at some private joke while one lit a fat cigar. Directly behind Longarm's and Cynthia's car was the stable car.

"Don't mind a little hay and straw, do you?" Longarm said as he dropped down the steps to the ground and then turned to reach up and wrap his hands around Cynthia's slender waist.

As he pulled her down off the platform and set her easily onto the railroad bed, she said, "You mean, you want to do it with a bunch of animals watching? I absolutely love the idea, you naughty, naughty man!"

"Come on!"

He grabbed her hand and, looking around to make sure no one saw them stealing off together like oversexed schoolchildren, led her back to the stable car. He looked around once more to make sure no one was watching. The engineers were too busy feeding water to the locomotive and the brakemen were too involved in their joke to worry about Longarm and Cynthia.

Quickly, Longarm slid the stable car door open.

"Here we go," he said, lifting her up through the open door.

Cynthia giggled at the thrill of being tossed around so easily, as though she weighed no more than a ragdoll.

Longarm leaped up into the stock car, looked outside once more, and then quickly slid the door closed. The car was all brown shadows and blurred edges.

The only light was the slender columns of golden sunshine bleeding in between the car's vertical wall boards. Dust motes shone, drifting lazily. Horses nickered softly, shuffled around.

The Larimers' two-seater, leather buggy with high, red-spoked wheels sat a ways back in the shadows. The General had sent it along so that Cynthia and Mrs. Schimpelfinnig would have a stylish ride to the town of Arapaho, after they'd detrained in Cheyenne. Longarm would have the honor of driving them.

The only thing he was thinking about driving now was the General's daughter, who threw herself against him and wrapped her arms around his neck. Longarm wrapped his arms around her waist and kissed her long and deep, entangling his tongue with hers.

Cynthia moaned, returning the kiss, ramming her hot tongue against his, mashing her breasts against his chest, grinding her pelvis against his hips.

"Oh, Lord, you're ready for me, aren't you?" she said, lowering a hand to his bulging crotch.

"My dear," Longarm said, "I've been ready for you since about ten minutes after the last time we parted."

Cynthia's lower jaw dropped in shock. "Custis, I think

that's the most romantic thing I've ever heard any man say to any woman."

"Ah, hell."

"No, I mean it." Cynthia rose up onto her tiptoes and mashed her lips against his. "Fuck me."

"That's what we're here for, ain't it?"

She laughed in wicked delight and lowered her hands to the buckle of his cartridge belt. When she'd removed the gun belt, letting it drop to the floor of the stable car, she immediately, deftly went to work on the belt holding his whipcord trousers up his lean hips, and then she opened the buttons of his fly.

She peeled his pants open, reached into the fly of his summer-weight underwear, and pulled out his fully erect cock. She knelt before him as though in worship, crossed her eyes as she stared at the impressive shaft standing up proud and hard and angling back against his belly.

"I've been thinking about this ax handle for months now," Cynthia said, wrapping a hand around the massive, banana-shaped organ and pumping him gently. "Oh, Custis, no man can please me like you can!"

"Feelin's mutual, there, girl," Longarm said, grimacing as she closed her tender lips over the head of the swollen member.

Looking up at him from under her thin, black brows, she slowly slid her mouth down on him. Her mouth opened wider, wider, her lips feeling like warm, moist silk sliding over his member.

Longarm groaned.

As she continued to slide her mouth down him, she flicked her tongue across the underside of his cock, antagonizing him, sending several lances of fiery desire through his loins.

His heart hiccupped.

Longarm rocked back on the heels of his boots as she went down as far as she could, gagging slightly, and then slid her mouth back to the engorged, purple, mushroom head. She licked him like a fruit-flavored sucker again, pausing only to giggle at his groans and sighs, and then sucked him harder for a time, until she knew from experience that she had him about halfway to his precipice.

"Oh, take me, now, Custis. Fuck me in the hay, please—with the horses!"

She rose, chuckled, grabbed his bobbing member, and led him into a stall where the Larimers' Hanoverian, trained for pulling the Larimer surrey, stood eyeing the lovers skeptically, wagging its tail and twitching an ear.

"Hello, Thunder," Cynthia said as she ducked under the roped stall. She kissed the horse's long snout, patting its wither, before Longarm swept the girl into his arms, swung around, and dropped to his knees. He lay her out in a mound of hay in a corner of the stall and slid her dress up her legs.

"Fuck me." The girl groaned, writhing in the hay as though enduring the most excruciating agony. "Oh, fuck me, please, Custis. I've been dreaming about you for months now—remembering how you plundered me with that massive organ of yours in Uncle's garden shed! Do you remember? While Aunt May was serving tea to her friends from the opera company?"

"What the hell?" Longarm ran his hands up and down Cynthia's long, smooth, creamy bare legs. "You ain't wearin' no under frillies, Miss Cynthia."

Cynthia smiled and chewed her thumbnail. "I came prepared for you."

"You mean, you been ridin' right across from me in that seat beside old Aunt Beatrice with *nothin' on under your dress?*"

Cynthia tittered and continued to chew her thumbnail.

"Bad girl!"

"Punish me, Custis."

As Longarm slid her dress up around her waist, laying the entire length of her porcelain-pale legs bare down to her ankle-high, puce-colored, side-button shoes, she lifted her legs and spread her knees wide.

"Oh, punish me!"

She reached up with both hands, grabbing her ankles, opening herself even wider, until she looked like a halved peach spread before him.

The petal-pink love hole enswathed by silky black fur opened like a mouth, extending its tiny tongue that appeared as erect as Longarm's massive, nodding shaft. Cynthia groaned, scowled down between them at the member in question, which he lowered ever so slowly to the girl's open, waiting pussy.

"Fuck me, fuck me, fuck me," she cooed, wrapping a hand around him and sliding the swollen mushroom head up and down her slit.

Longarm sighed as the feeling of dipping his dong in warm mud engulfed him and caused his loins to throb. Cynthia drew a long breath, lifted her head, and closed her mouth over his as she pressed the head of his cock inside her.

Longarm kissed her vehemently, passionately, as he

slid the organ deeper, lowering his hips to hers. At the same time, keeping his mouth clamped against her own, he pushed her head back in the hay.

And then he was bottomed out inside the girl, grinding his hips against hers, and she was groaning deep in her chest, hooking her bare legs around him and grinding her heels against his ass while he slammed against her over and over.

Cynthia groaned and whimpered, shaking her head and occasionally lifting it to look down between them at his cock driving in and out of her black-tufted, pink-petaled snatch. Longarm propped himself on his arms, his knees planted in the straw between the girl's spread legs. He went to work in earnest, pummeling away at the wanton creature, Cynthia's knees flapping like wings to each side of him.

He could feel the heels of her shoes grinding into his ass. This enflamed him even more.

As they toiled together, Cynthia unbuttoned her dress and peeled it open so that her large, full, pale breasts flopped naked between them. Longarm lowered his head to her cleavage and slid his nose and mustache up and down that deep, mysterious valley. While continuing to fuck her hard, driving her deeper and deeper into the straw, he kneaded one breast while nuzzling and licking the other one.

Both nipples pebbled, swelled, distended.

"Oh!" Cynthia said. "Oh, Custis—oh, *gawd*, Custis!"

Longarm lifted his head from her magnificent left tit but kept squeezing the other. He arched his back and gritted his teeth, driving even harder and faster.

"Oh!" the girl said, louder. "Oh! Oh! Oh, *fuck*!"

She arched her own back, ground the back of her head into the straw, gritting her teeth until the cords stood out in her long, fine neck. Longarm clamped a hand over her mouth, knowing from experience that she couldn't control herself when she came, and then rose up on the toes of his boots for better leverage.

He drove deep and held there at base of her womb.

He exploded inside her, red lights flashing behind his squeezed-shut eyelids. Bells tolled in his head. His heart throbbed in his temples until he thought his head would burst.

He could feel Cynthia's warm lips and open mouth against the palm of his hand. Her tongue ground against it. The girl shuddered beneath him, bucked, grunted, rammed her shoes into his ass, convulsed.

Her warm honey bled out around his cock and coated his balls.

Longarm pulled out and then rammed himself back inside the beautiful heiress as he continued to spend himself, his seed still jetting though the convulsions were diminishing gradually. When they stopped altogether, his muscles turned to putty, and he dropped on top of her with a long, ragged sigh. Her breasts were sandwiched between them.

The sound of crunching gravel was heard outside the car. There was a light knock on the stable car door. Beatrice Schimpelfinnig said, "Cynthia? Deputy? Are you *in* there?"

Chapter 3

The next day, as Longarm drove the Larimers' fancy, canopied carriage up into the foothills of the Buckskin Hills northwest of Cheyenne, Cynthia called from the seat behind his driver's perch, "Custis, would you mind stopping the carriage, please, and pulling off the trail?"

Longarm glanced over his shoulder. Cynthia was riding in the carriage's quilted leather seat beside Aunt Beatrice, who looked especially puffy and drawn. Apparently, the three-hour ride along the rough wagon trail through the high, sage- and yucca-stippled desert ringed with dramatic mountains had been a little rough on the old gal.

"Why would I want to do that?" Longarm said, feigning innocence.

Cynthia held his gaze with a crisp, faintly admonishing one of her own. Mrs. Schimpelfinnig gave him the same look, hardening her jaws and flaring her nostrils.

Longarm grinned with boyish deviltry out one side of his mouth. He couldn't help needling the woman a little. He and Cynthia had managed to avoid getting caught with their pants down in the stable car by remaining very quiet until the woman had given up and walked on, calling for the conductor to help her open the door.

When she'd passed, Longarm and Cynthia had snuck out of the car and back into the coach car, acting as nonchalant and devil-may-care as possible despite the hay and straw that had tickled the lawman's ass all the way to Cheyenne.

But if Mrs. Schimpelfinnig had been suspicious of them before their stable car escapade, she was even more so now. In fact, since they'd left Cheyenne early that morning after spending the previous night in the Union Pacific Hotel, Longarm had felt the old woman's eyes burning twin holes into the back of his head. She'd let him know very quietly but in no uncertain terms that she'd be keeping her eagle eyes on him and her most precious niece for the remainder of the trip.

"Oh, sure, sure—I understand," Longarm said, turning the Hanoverian off the right side of the trail and into the shade of some cottonwoods lining a creek. "It just hasn't been all that long since we stopped *last* time, so, you know, I was just sorta wonderin'."

"Please keep your wondering to yourself, Deputy Long," Mrs. Schimpelfinnig admonished as Longarm drew back on the horse's reins.

Apparently, the old woman's bladder was a little logy though Longarm reckoned anyone's bladder would get logy if they drank as much coffee as Mrs. Schimpelfinnig had drank that morning before they'd pulled away from the hotel after breakfasting in the stately Union Pacific Dining Room. She'd brought an extra jug and a pile of doughnuts along for the ride, and within the trip's first hour she'd consumed all the coffee and doughnuts herself.

Longarm made a mental note, inwardly chuckling, to stay upwind of the old gal.

He set the carriage's brake and then helped the old woman down and gave her the carpet accordion bag she always hauled off on one of her "walks." As she started to amble away, she glanced back over her stout shoulder and said, "I'll be back shortly. Not going far." This last she spat out at Longarm, as though to say, "So don't try anything, bucko!"

"You're a devil," Cynthia said when her aunt was out of hearing, ranging around in the trees for a private shrub.

"That mean you don't think we'd best risk a quick poke in the buggy? Might take her a while. It did last time."

"Don't tempt me."

"Why not? *I'm* tempted."

Cynthia glanced in the direction in which her aunt had disappeared, and then stepped up close to Longarm, pressing her belly against his groin. "Didn't yesterday hold you?"

"Did it hold you?"

"No, but you know I'm an absolute maniac for you, Custis." She reached up and placed both her hands lightly on his leathery brown cheeks, running both index fingers down into his thick longhorn mustache. "Maybe we should think about making this a permanent thing—you and me?"

"Maybe," Longarm said, taking her hands in his and

kissing them. "If I was a few years younger and independently wealthy. I got me a feelin' the Larimers wouldn't appreciate havin' a workaday gent mixin' in with all that pedigreed blood."

"Maybe not, but we'd have quite a time—you and me."

Longarm couldn't help narrowing an incredulous eye at her. Never before, during the past three years they'd been "friends," had either one ever brought up the prospect of marriage. Longarm had always thought it was obvious they couldn't be together for the long, serious run. He'd thought she'd realized the same thing. Besides, knowing that they couldn't ever be together as a married couple had made their rare, strenuous, and furtive carnal adventures all the more precious.

"Oh, don't give me that look, Custis. I'm just thinking out loud. I guess it's just that Casey's imminent wedding has gotten me thinking about . . . eventually settling down."

"You? Cynthia, you can't cage that tiger inside you. There ain't no way to do that and keep that tiger happy."

"I'm not getting any younger."

"You're only twenty-three, darlin'."

Cynthia hiked a shoulder. "To some, I'm an old maid. Aunt May and Aunt Beatrice are always asking me if I haven't met someone by now. You know—someone I'd like to settle down with."

She looked at Longarm askance, a tad bit abashed. "I reckon you're the only one I'd even consider, Custis."

Longarm glanced around to make sure that Mrs. Schimpelfinnig wasn't shuffling toward them, and then engulfed the girl in his arms. "You just haven't found the right one yet. You will, sooner or later. Some prince over the big ocean yonder, no doubt. You know enough of them."

"Oh, I know enough of them, of course." Cynthia wrapped her arms around Longarm's waist and returned his hug. "And of course a few have proposed, but damnit, Custis, I just don't feel the spark for any of them." She pulled away and walked into the trees. "My friend Casey just looked and sounded so happy the last time I saw her in Denver, when she told me about the young man she was marrying."

Longarm reached inside his frock coat and dug a cheroot from his shirt pocket. "Hard to believe any gal you know would be marryin' a badge toter."

Cynthia leaned back against a boulder and slid a vagrant lock of black hair back from her right eye. "Casey had a falling out with her mother after her father died. Her father was a good friend of my uncle's. Anyway, she decided to go off to a teaching college in Kansas City, and she met a young soldier on the train. They corresponded for a year, and then the soldier visited her in Kansas City and proposed."

"Her family didn't have anything to say about that?"

"Nothing that Casey listened to. If you think I'm headstrong . . . well, Casey could teach me a few things." Cynthia chuckled and crossed her arms on her breasts. "She was so angry about what her mother had to say about her future husband, whom Mrs. Summerville had never met, that she told her mother to take her out of the family will. So, Casey gave up her family's fortune to marry the dashing young soldier who was about to be appointed sheriff of Arapaho and the surrounding county by his father, whom you, coincidentally, know, my dear Custis."

"If young Ryan is anything like his father, old Thrum, he's quite a catch. I just hope Casey realizes how comparatively frugal she'll be living, compared to how she was raised." Longarm scratched a lucifer to life on his holster and touched the flame to the three-for-a-nickel cheroot.

"I have a feeling Casey and Ryan will do just fine. Love can make up for a lot, you know." Cynthia dropped her eyes, pensive, and then lifted them to Longarm. Lines cut into the bridge of her nose as she canted her head to one side and asked, "Don't you think, Custis?"

The lawman puffed his cheroot and looked off, suddenly uncomfortable with the conversation. "Wouldn't know."

Cynthia pushed away from her rock and walked toward him. She placed her hands on his forearms and looked up at him from beneath her straw hat. "This is a question I never expected to ask you, Custis. It's one that I hoped I'd never feel compelled to ask, because I thought it might complicate things between us, might temper some of the nasty excitement of our . . . trysts. But . . . do you—?"

"Yes," he said before she could even finish.

He smiled down at her. "But let's leave it at that, shall we? Since there's really no point in taking the conversation further—me bein' who I am and you bein' who you are."

Cynthia rose on her tiptoes and planted a tender kiss on his lips. "Touché, my dear Longarm. Touché."

A branch snapped in the direction in which Mrs. Schimpelfinnig had disappeared. Cynthia stepped back from Longarm, and they both turned to see the old

woman stumbling toward them through the grass growing up around the cottonwoods, her accordion carpetbag
slung over one stout shoulder.

She appeared flushed and out of breath.

"Are you all right, Aunt Beatrice?" Cynthia asked,
walking over, taking the woman's arm and leading her
to the carriage.

"I'm fine, dear. I could do with something to eat, however, and a wee bit more coffee. The trip in this wretched
buggy—you know how I hate long trips by carriage—is
growing rather tiresome." Mrs. Schimpelfinnig cast a
cool, baldly reproving glance at Longarm and pitched
her voice with peevishness. "How long before we arrive
at Arapaho, Deputy Long?"

"It's just over the next . . ." Longarm glanced toward
the northwest and let his voice trail off. He frowned at
what appeared a tendril of charcoal-gray smoke rising
between two cone-shaped bluffs.

"What is it?" Cynthia asked as she helped her aunt
into the carriage.

"Looks like a fire up near Arapaho."

"Fire?"

"Probably just someone burnin' a field or some dead
brush." Longarm glanced once more at the smoke and
then offered his hand to Cynthia. When she was seated
beside her aunt, both women shielding their eyes with
their hands and staring toward the smoke, Longarm
climbed into the driver's seat, released the brake, and
pulled the Hanoverian onto the trail.

While the smart-stepping sorrel pulled the carriage
up toward the pass between the buttes, Longarm held his
gaze on the smoke. The closer the carriage drew to the

low pass, the smoke column widened, grew bushier. Longarm felt fingers of unease tickle his backbone.

Where there was smoke, as the saying went, there was fire. He hoped the fire was far afield of Arapaho. Fires in dry, western towns spread as fast as those that plowed through a mountainside of dead timber. Longarm had seen more than his share of fire-gutted or decimated settlements, and none of them had been pretty.

The Hanoverian trotted up and over the top of the pass. As it started down the other side, Arapaho spread out in a bowl in the low, piñon- and cedar-stippled hills and high bluffs to the west—a mile or so from the base of the pass. Behind Longarm, Cynthia drew a sharp breath.

"Oh, my goodness!" exclaimed Mrs. Schimpelfinnig. "The town's on fire!"

Longarm hoorawed the fine horse in the traces, sending it barreling down the pass. As the carriage bounced over chuckholes and hammered over small rocks, the lawman stared at the column of black smoke and flames rising from what appeared the town's center. As the horse closed on the small settlement, Longarm saw that the fire appeared to involve a large building on the main street's right side.

He could see no scurry of movement around the building in question, which seemed odd. Usually, a bucket brigade would have been formed between the town's main water supply and the conflagration, and men would be running and yelling as they passed the buckets.

But then the lawman started to understand. And he didn't like it a bit.

For beneath the drumming of the Hanoverian's

hooves, the hammering of the buggy's wheels, and the squawking of the leather thoroughbraces, he heard the rataplan of what could only have been gunfire.

"Ah, shit!" Longarm stood up in the driver's box and whipped the reins over the horse's back, encouraging even more speed.

All hell was breaking loose in Arapaho.

epped away from the drugstore's front
is own Winchester straight out from his
h quiet, commanding menace, he said,
r. I'm a deputy U.S. marshal. Toss down
face me."

topped dead in his tracks, facing the street.
to stop breathing for a moment. A half sec-
widened his eyes and gritted his teeth as he
'd Longarm, leveling his carbine,and loudly
shell into the action.

fired twice, his Winchester crashing loudly
alley, his empty cartridge casings pinging
ardwalk behind him.

red a fresh shell into the firing chamber and
he hard case trigger his own rifle into the
he stumbled back against the wall behind him.
nted as he dropped the rifle and tried to get his
ath him to no avail. One foot slipped out from
h and he fell back against the wall and slid down
ound, where he lay on his side, shaking.
arm took a knee, looking around.

he realized that the hard case he'd shot had likely
ing to slip around behind the men shooting from
osite side of the main street, from in front of a
ore about a block up from Longarm's position.
neant at least one of those fellas was a lawman—
y Thrum's son, Ryan, who'd taken over the local
gging job from his father about a month ago, due
rum's latest heart attack.

e men on the side of the law were throwing inter-
nt spurts of lead at a building just up the street from

Chapter 4

Longarm could smell the smoke from the fire. He could
hear the shooting clearly now. Men were shouting angrily.
A dog was barking anxiously, and a baby was crying.

The edge of the town was a hundred yards away. As
the Hanoverian pulled the carriage around the last bend,
Longarm hauled back on the reins. The horse stopped
under some scraggly aspens. The aspens and a large boulder shielded the carriage from town.

Longarm set the brake and dropped to the ground.

"You ladies stay here," he ordered, jogging to the rear
of the carriage, where their luggage was stored in a rack.

"Oh, Lord! Oh, Lord!" intoned Mrs. Schimpelfinnig.
She stood up in the carriage and was staring through the
trees toward town. "That's shooting, isn't it? Oh, Lord!
I knew this trip was a mistake, Cynthia. Out here there
are no laws except the law of the gun! These backwater
settlements are populated by *owlhoots*!"

"Aunt Beatrice, please sit down!"

"Ma'am, I going to have to ask you to sit down," Longarm said, sliding his prized Winchester '73 from its leather scabbard and tossing the scabbard back into the luggage rack.

"Lawless, I tell you!" chortled Cynthia's stout aunt. "Deputy Long, I demand that you turn this carriage around this very instant and take us back to the train at Cheyenne!"

"Ma'am, we're a good ways out of town, so you shouldn't be in any trouble, but I'm not going to guarantee that if you don't take a seat, you won't get your head blown off!"

Cynthia was tugging on the heavy woman's arm. "Aunt Beatrice, please sit down!" She whipped her anxious gaze to Longarm. "Custis, what's happening?"

"I don't know, but I'm going to find out." Longarm pumped a cartridge into the Winchester's magazine, off cocked the hammer, and set the barrel on his right shoulder. "You stay here with your aunt. When I think it's safe for you to enter the town, I'll come back for you. Until then, you both stay here and keep your heads down!"

With that he bounded forward along the trail, running as fast as his long legs could take him.

"Custis, be careful!" Cynthia yelled behind him.

As Longarm rounded the bend and approached the town, he could see down the main street, which was merely an extension of the trail he was on.

He'd been right. The building that was on fire was on the town's right side, about halfway down the street—a corner building that appeared constructed of pink sandstone. Since the building, excepting its shake-shingled mansard roof, was stone, the fire likely wouldn't spread

as quickly to the
from flames spitti
contained.

The shooting se
of the street near th
see smoke puffing f
street's left side and
another building on tl
dog stood between L
boardwalk, staring tov
wagging its tail and bar

Longarm slowed his p
building at his end of the
He had to size up the situat
ing at whom, as best he co
head shot off. Only then
trouble.

He stepped onto a boardv
store. Someone jerked a shad
his right, and he heard quick t
ried into hiding. Longarm co
the roofed boardwalk fronting
was almost to the building's oth
jerked back, pressing his shoulde
front wall.

He edged a look around the co
beyond. A man was walking up the
street—a tall man in a high-crow
spruce-green duster, and high-toppe
spurs. He had two pistols on his hip
in his gloved hands.

A curly wolf, if Longarm had ever

Longarm s
wall, aiming
right hip. Wi
"Hold it, fell
that rifle and

The man s
He appeared
ond later he
swung towa
ramming a

Longarm
around the
onto the bo

He leve
watched t
ground as

He gru
feet bene
under hir
to the gr

Long
Soon
been try
the opp
feed st
That m
possib
lawdo
to Th
Th
mitte

Longarm. Judging by the shots, he thought there were five guns being fired—three on the street's right side, two on its left side, where the townsmen were hunkered down behind a stock trough.

Longarm hoped he was right about who was who, because at the rate the pink building was burning and due to spread, he had to work fast in helping the lawman or whoever was holding off the curly wolves. He stepped out into the alley where the dead man lay, and then walked down the gap to his right, intending to get around the other three outlaws.

He shouldered up to the side of the building on the alley's far side, doffed his hat, and edged a look around the rear. All clear. Donning his hat, he hurried around the corner and began long-striding toward the building from which the outlaws were firing. He thought it was the third one to the west.

The thought had no sooner swept through his brain than a man stepped out a back door of the very building that Longarm was heading for. Longarm stopped. The other man stopped. He was small and young, wearing a broad-brimmed tan hat. Two pistols were tied low on his hips. The eyes shaded by the hat brim were set close together, and they had a sharp, menacing light in them.

He was carrying a Henry rifle down low by his side. Now, holding Longarm's gaze, he slowly began to raise the rifle.

"Uh-uh," Longarm said. "You don't wanna do that, young fella. I'm a federal lawman."

As if to show Longarm how wrong he was, the kid gave an angry, bellowing wail and snapped his rifle up, cocking it. Longarm shot him twice in the chest, lifting him off his feet and throwing him several yards straight back. His body hit the ground, and the rifle clattered down beside him a half a second later.

Longarm broke into a dead run, quickly covering the ground between him and the building the kid had come out of. The rear door was open. Longarm sidled up to the back of the wood-frame building, stepped up to the door, doffed his hat, and edged a peek inside. He couldn't see much in the dense shadows, but he could hear men shouting and shooting from the front of the place—a shop of some kind.

He doffed his hat and hurried into the rear room, slid a curtain aside from a doorway, and peered into what looked like a woman's dress shop, with wooden mannequins standing here and there, wearing the latest in ladies' fashions, and bolts of cloth leaning in racks. Longarm stared past a counter to his left toward the front of the store, where three men were hunkered down by three broken-out windows.

One was just now shooting two pistols through the window nearest the closed door and shouting, "Best let us on out of here, McIntyre. You don't, and we'll burn it down!"

Near the outlaw, a middle-aged woman in a crisp green-and-gold-brocade dress trimmed with white lace lay dead in a pool of her own blood, glassy eyes staring at the ceiling. Broken window glass was scattered over and around the woman.

The dead woman kindled a fire inside of Longarm. He stepped through the curtained doorway and dropped to a knee at the end of the counter. He could see only one of the shooters clearly—the one who'd just fired and was now

Chapter 4

Longarm could smell the smoke from the fire. He could hear the shooting clearly now. Men were shouting angrily. A dog was barking anxiously, and a baby was crying.

The edge of the town was a hundred yards away. As the Hanoverian pulled the carriage around the last bend, Longarm hauled back on the reins. The horse stopped under some scraggly aspens. The aspens and a large boulder shielded the carriage from town.

Longarm set the brake and dropped to the ground.

"You ladies stay here," he ordered, jogging to the rear of the carriage, where their luggage was stored in a rack.

"Oh, Lord! Oh, Lord!" intoned Mrs. Schimpelfinnig. She stood up in the carriage and was staring through the trees toward town. "That's shooting, isn't it? Oh, Lord! I knew this trip was a mistake, Cynthia. Out here there are no laws except the law of the gun! These backwater settlements are populated by *owlhoots*!"

"Aunt Beatrice, please sit down!"

"Ma'am, I going to have to ask you to sit down," Long-arm said, sliding his prized Winchester '73 from its leather scabbard and tossing the scabbard back into the luggage rack.

"Lawless, I tell you!" chortled Cynthia's stout aunt. "Deputy Long, I demand that you turn this carriage around this very instant and take us back to the train at Cheyenne!"

"Ma'am, we're a good ways out of town, so you shouldn't be in any trouble, but I'm not going to guarantee that if you don't take a seat, you won't get your head blown off!"

Cynthia was tugging on the heavy woman's arm. "Aunt Beatrice, please sit down!" She whipped her anxious gaze to Longarm. "Custis, what's happening?"

"I don't know, but I'm going to find out." Longarm pumped a cartridge into the Winchester's magazine, off cocked the hammer, and set the barrel on his right shoulder. "You stay here with your aunt. When I think it's safe for you to enter the town, I'll come back for you. Until then, you both stay here and keep your heads down!"

With that he bounded forward along the trail, running as fast as his long legs could take him.

"Custis, be careful!" Cynthia yelled behind him.

As Longarm rounded the bend and approached the town, he could see down the main street, which was merely an extension of the trail he was on.

He'd been right. The building that was on fire was on the town's right side, about halfway down the street—a corner building that appeared constructed of pink sandstone. Since the building, excepting its shake-shingled mansard roof, was stone, the fire likely wouldn't spread as quickly to the other buildings around it. So far, aside from flames spitting from the windows, it seemed to be contained.

The shooting seemed to be coming from both sides of the street near the burning building. Longarm could see smoke puffing from behind a stock trough on the street's left side and from the broken-out windows of another building on the right. A medium-sized spotted dog stood between Longarm and the shooters, on a boardwalk, staring toward the commotion, anxiously wagging its tail and barking its fool head off.

Longarm slowed his pace as he angled toward the first building at his end of the town, on the street's right side. He had to size up the situation, figure out who was shooting at whom, as best he could without getting his own head shot off. Only then could he try to defuse the trouble.

He stepped onto a boardwalk fronting a small drugstore. Someone jerked a shade down over a window to his right, and he heard quick footsteps as someone hurried into hiding. Longarm continued forward along the roofed boardwalk fronting the drugstore. When he was almost to the building's other side, he stopped and jerked back, pressing his shoulder against the drugstore's front wall.

He edged a look around the corner and into the alley beyond. A man was walking up the alley toward the main street—a tall man in a high-crowned brown Stetson, spruce-green duster, and high-topped, brown boots with spurs. He had two pistols on his hips and a Winchester in his gloved hands.

A curly wolf, if Longarm had ever seen one.

Longarm stepped away from the drugstore's front wall, aiming his own Winchester straight out from his right hip. With quiet, commanding menace, he said, "Hold it, feller. I'm a deputy U.S. marshal. Toss down that rifle and face me."

The man stopped dead in his tracks, facing the street. He appeared to stop breathing for a moment. A half second later he widened his eyes and gritted his teeth as he swung toward Longarm, leveling his carbine, and loudly ramming a shell into the action.

Longarm fired twice, his Winchester crashing loudly around the alley, his empty cartridge casings pinging onto the boardwalk behind him.

He levered a fresh shell into the firing chamber and watched the hard case trigger his own rifle into the ground as he stumbled back against the wall behind him.

He grunted as he dropped the rifle and tried to get his feet beneath him to no avail. One foot slipped out from under him and he fell back against the wall and slid down to the ground, where he lay on his side, shaking.

Longarm took a knee, looking around.

Soon he realized that the hard case he'd shot had likely been trying to slip around behind the men shooting from the opposite side of the main street, from in front of a feed store about a block up from Longarm's position. That meant at least one of those fellas was a lawman— possibly Thrum's son, Ryan, who'd taken over the local lawdogging job from his father about a month ago, due to Thrum's latest heart attack.

The men on the side of the law were throwing intermittent spurts of lead at a building just up the street from

Longarm. Judging by the shots, he thought there were five guns being fired—three on the street's right side, two on its left side, where the townsmen were hunkered down behind a stock trough.

Longarm hoped he was right about who was who, because at the rate the pink building was burning and due to spread, he had to work fast in helping the lawman or whoever was holding off the curly wolves. He stepped out into the alley where the dead man lay, and then walked down the gap to his right, intending to get around the other three outlaws.

He shouldered up to the side of the building on the alley's far side, doffed his hat, and edged a look around the rear. All clear. Donning his hat, he hurried around the corner and began long-striding toward the building from which the outlaws were firing. He thought it was the third one to the west.

The thought had no sooner swept through his brain than a man stepped out a back door of the very building that Longarm was heading for. Longarm stopped. The other man stopped. He was small and young, wearing a broad-brimmed tan hat. Two pistols were tied low on his hips. The eyes shaded by the hat brim were set close together, and they had a sharp, menacing light in them.

He was carrying a Henry rifle down low by his side. Now, holding Longarm's gaze, he slowly began to raise the rifle.

"Uh-uh," Longarm said. "You don't wanna do that, young fella. I'm a federal lawman."

As if to show Longarm how wrong he was, the kid gave an angry, bellowing wail and snapped his rifle up, cocking it. Longarm shot him twice in the chest, lifting him off his feet and throwing him several yards straight back. His body hit the ground, and the rifle clattered down beside him a half a second later.

Longarm broke into a dead run, quickly covering the ground between him and the building the kid had come out of. The rear door was open. Longarm sidled up to the back of the wood-frame building, stepped up to the door, doffed his hat, and edged a peek inside. He couldn't see much in the dense shadows, but he could hear men shouting and shooting from the front of the place—a shop of some kind.

He doffed his hat and hurried into the rear room, slid a curtain aside from a doorway, and peered into what looked like a woman's dress shop, with wooden mannequins standing here and there, wearing the latest in ladies' fashions, and bolts of cloth leaning in racks. Longarm stared past a counter to his left toward the front of the store, where three men were hunkered down by three broken-out windows.

One was just now shooting two pistols through the window nearest the closed door and shouting, "Best let us on out of here, McIntyre. You don't, and we'll burn it down!"

Near the outlaw, a middle-aged woman in a crisp green-and-gold-brocade dress trimmed with white lace lay dead in a pool of her own blood, glassy eyes staring at the ceiling. Broken window glass was scattered over and around the woman.

The dead woman kindled a fire inside of Longarm. He stepped through the curtained doorway and dropped to a knee at the end of the counter. He could see only one of the shooters clearly—the one who'd just fired and was now sitting on the floor with his back against the front wall, punching fresh cartridges into one of his two pistols.

Blood oozed from a bullet burn on his right cheek.

Longarm pressed his Winchester's stock against his shoulder and drew a bead on the outlaw. He shouted, "Hold it there, you son of a bitch. Custis Long, U.S. marshal!"

He was pleased as punch when the outlaw did not heed his warning but shot a fiery-eyed, startled gaze at him and snapped up one of his pistols. The outlaw didn't get a single shot off before Longarm's Winchester roared, punching a .44-caliber slug through the dead center of his forehead and painting the wall behind him with chunks of white brain and gobs of red blood.

"What the hell?" one of the other men shouted, whipping around.

Longarm threw himself to the floor in front of the counter as a rifle cracked three times quickly. The slug chewed through bolts of cloth or thumped into the front of the counter.

"Someone snuck up on us from behind, Bristol!" shouted the man who'd just fired.

Longarm rose, rammed his rifle between two bolts of cloth, planted a bead on the chest of a man moving toward him and crouching over an old Spencer carbine. The man saw the rifle barrel and widened his eyes. Before he could snap the carbine up, Longarm drilled three rounds through his chest.

The man screamed, dropped his rifle, and stumbled backward, pinwheeling, before he fell through the large, broken-out middle front window and out onto the boardwalk.

Another man ran toward Longarm, screaming and triggering two pistols. Longarm dropped to the floor and scrambled around behind the display holding the bolts of cloth. The shooter's pistols blazed away at where Longarm had been, causing shredded cloth to rain amidst a thick, peppery cloud of powder smoke.

Longarm hunkered down between the end of the display and the front counter, quickly, quietly shoving fresh cartridges into his Winchester's loading gate. The last outlaw was still triggering led into the bolts around Longarm, yelling, "You're gonna die you federal badge–totin' son of a bitch!"

Longarm heard one of the man's pistols click, empty.

There was another tinny click.

The man said, "Shit!"

Longarm rose to his feet and swung around the opposite side of the bolt cloth display. The shooter—a short, paunchy man in a ragged yellow shirt and brown chaps—stood staring at him, hang-jawed in shock. Longarm rammed his Winchester's brass butt plate against the short killer's forehead, and the man stumbled backward, twisted around, and fell to his hands and knees, groaning.

Longarm stepped forward, rammed his right boot toe against the man's ass, driving him to the floor where he lay, groaning and whimpering, half conscious.

Longarm dropped to a knee beside the man and looked through the broken-out windows. The shooting had stopped. An incredulous silence hung over the street. Wisps of black smoke and ashes billowed in front of the windows.

Longarm shouted, "Hold your fire, fellas! Custis Long, deputy U.S. marshal! I believe they're done for!"

Out in the street, aside from the barking dog, there was only silence. Longarm spied movement, however. A man rose from behind the stock trough on the street's other side, kitty-corner from the ladies' dress shop.

Longarm grabbed the back of the injured hard case's collar and jerked the man across the shop to the front door, which was closed. He opened the door, kicking the groaning man through it and onto the boardwalk fronting the shop, and turned to face the street, ready to seek cover if some nervous townsman triggered a shot at him.

He recognized the man walking toward him as Thrum McIntyre, former sheriff of Platte County. Longarm didn't say anything.

He was taken aback by the man's shocked, haggard expression as he angled across the street to Longarm's right. McIntyre was a tall, lanky man in a cream shirt and brown vest, wavy silver hair dropping from his brown Stetson to brush his shirt collar. His weathered face was craggy and hung from the cheekbones like individual swatches of time-yellowed leather. His soup-strainer mustache was the same silver as his hair.

Time had been hard on the aging lawman. His shoulders and hips were pointy, and he leaned forward as though against a heavy burden.

Scowling his bewilderment, Longarm followed the old lawman with his eyes. McIntyre crouched over a man lying in the street to Longarm's right. The marshal placed a hand on the fallen man's shoulder, and then turned to yell at the aproned men stepping warily out of their shops, most holding rifles or shotguns, and at the cow-boys moving out of the saloons.

"Grab some buckets!" McIntyre shouted, waving a bent arm toward the burning building that Longarm now saw was a bank. "Form a brigade. Get that fire doused before it spreads! Some of you fellas fetch shovels and start throwin' dirt!"

As though in a trance, McIntire then returned his gaze to the fallen man before him.

Longarm looked around. In the street before the bank lay two other men—one near the stock trough behind which McIntyre had taken cover, another on the board-walk fronting a saloon. Apparently, the cutthroats had robbed the bank, and the fallen were men the robbers had cut down as they'd tried to get away.

Seeing that the trouble aside from the fire was over, and that men were now scurrying toward a well up the street to the west, Longarm walked over to where McIntyre was just now rolling the fallen man before him onto his back. The fallen man was young—maybe mid-twenties. A handsome young man with sandy hair and a dark sandy mustache.

His pale blue eyes were half open. He was spiffily attired in a broadcloth suit with string tie, an empty hol-ster on his hip. A Colt Peacemaker lay in the street nearby.

The man's paisley-pattered vest under the dark suit-coat was blood matted. He'd taken at least two slugs to his chest. A bullet hole marred his otherwise hand-some face. A muddy pool of blood grew in the dirt beneath him.

"Ah, hell." Longarm heard the words choke out of

him. He knew without having to be told that the young man lying dead on the street before McIntyre was the old lawman's son, Ryan.

Thrum McIntyre's clawlike, brown hand shook as he lightly raked his fingers over his son's eyes, closing them.

Chapter 5

Longarm felt sick, his legs weak, as he walked over and crouched down beside his old friend, Thrum McIntyre. The old lawman knelt beside his dead son, the new sheriff of Platte County. He stared down at the boy, his face a mask of confusion and disbelief.

Longarm placed a hand on McIntyre's arm. The ex-sheriff jerked his gaze to Longarm as though startled, as though just now realizing that the federal lawman was here.

"They killed him, Custis. They killed my boy. He'd just taken over the job two weeks ago. I pinned that badge on his coat myself." McIntyre turned his gaze back to the dead young man before him and ran a hand across his own, gray mustache. "Now, he's gone."

"What happened, Thrum?"

In a steady, low, even voice, staring down at his son, McIntyre said, "They robbed the bank. Colt Drummond bunch. Musta just got out of the state pen. I put Drummond away for six years. Came back to rob the bank."

McIntyre looked at the burning bank. The townsmen and cowboys had formed several bucket lines and were using water from the well to try to douse the flames. The situation looked hopeless. They could only get the fire under control and save the ones around it. Fortunately, the bank was on its own lot, separated by a good thirty yards from any other structure.

"They set the fire on their way out. Someone musta yelled for Ryan. He was walking along the street with the girl he was about to marry. I seen 'em from the café yonder. Ryan didn't have a chance. The gang cut him down right here as they rode out of town. Me and several of the other fellas here in town laid into the bunch."

"There was more?"

"There was a good twenty-five, includin' Drummond himself. Filled up the whole damn street." McIntyre looked at the stocky gent sitting back against the front of the ladies' dress shop, looking dazed from the clubbing. "These five lost their horses during the shooting. We pinned 'em down in the shop."

Longarm looked around. "You said your son was walking with his future wife. Where is she?"

McIntyre shuttled his now fiery-eyed gaze from the stocky outlaw to Longarm. He hardened his jaws, grabbed the front of Longarm's coat in his fist, and clenched it. "They got her, Custis. They swept Miss Casey up out of the street when she was seein' to Ryan. Drummond himself threw her over his saddle and rode away with her. They was all howlin' like a pack of wild wolves!"

Longarm stared at the man in shock.

McIntyre looked at the stocky outlaw on the boardwalk behind the federal lawman. The former sheriff rose, his knees creaking stiffly, and walked over to the outlaw. McIntyre slid his Smith & Wesson from the holster he wore high on his right hip and clicked the hammer back.

He held the gun straight down as he mounted the boardwalk and stood with his long shadow angling over the bleary-eyed hard case. A large, purple goose egg was swelling on the man's forehead, where Longarm had brained him with his rifle.

"Where they headed?" McIntyre asked in a low, cold voice, his thumb caressing the cocked hammer of his pistol.

The hard case looked up at the tall, old man and raised one brow. "What's that?"

"You heard me. I seen 'em headin' south past the hotel, out toward Elk Creek. But I wanna know where he's headed *exactly*."

"Hell, I don't . . ."

The hard case let his voice trail off as McIntyre raised his Smith & Wesson, aiming it straight out from his shoulder at the pudgy hard case's unshaven face.

"Where?"

Longarm stood by McIntyre's dead son. He had a feeling he knew where the ex-lawman was going with this, but he had no jurisdiction in the matter, even if he'd wanted any. Which right now at this moment, he did not.

"Where?" McIntyre said, louder.

"I don't know where they're headed," the pudgy outlaw said tonelessly, staring up into the muzzle of the pistol aimed at his face.

"You got three seconds."

"Please, goddamnit, I don't know!" The outlaw held his hands up high above his head in supplication.

"One."

"I told ya, I don't know, ya crazy old coot!"

"Two."

The outlaw was sobbing now as he turned his desperate gaze to Longarm. "You gotta stop this man. I'm in your custody. I'm *injured*!"

"Three."

"The Never Summers! A cabin in the Never Summers!" The outlaw lowered his head and raised his hands higher, squeezing his eyes closed. "Old Ranch on Purgatory Creek! Now get that pistol out of my face, goddamn your old stringy hide!"

McIntyre said with chilling evenness and menace, "If you're lyin', you murdering bastard, it'll just get all the hotter where I'm about to send you."

The outlaw jerked his shocked gaze back to the ex-lawman. "I done told you what you wanted to know!" he screamed. "Now, put that—"

Longarm tasted sour bile in the back of his throat as McIntyre's pistol thundered, blowing out the outlaw's right eye. The outlaw's head jerked backward and bounced off the wall behind him.

McIntyre's pistol blew out the killer's other eye, and the killer sagged onto one shoulder at the base of the ladies' clothing shop. Killing an unarmed prisoner in cold blood went against everything Longarm stood for as a lawman. But in this case, and for his friend who'd just lost his son on the young man's wedding day, Longarm was willing to make an exception.

McIntyre lowered the smoking Smith & Wesson. As

he turned to Longarm, his face was ashen. His knees seemed to weaken and he stumbled backward. Worried that his old friend was having another heart attack, Longarm ran up onto the boardwalk and wrapped an arm around the older man's waist.

"Easy, Thrum. Take it easy. Best sit down—you ain't lookin' too good."

"Ain't feelin' too good." McIntyre sat down at the edge of the boardwalk, his long legs curled in the street. He leaned back against an awning support post, dug a white handkerchief out of his pocket, and mopped his sweaty, pale brow. "Never done nothin' like what I just did."

"I know you didn't. It's all right. As far as I'm concerned, anyone asks, he was pullin' a hideout."

"Killed my . . . son." McIntyre shifted his sickly gaze to where the young county sheriff lay did in the street. "Just like that, they killed him. Took his bride to be . . . on their weddin' day."

"I'll get her back."

"We will."

"Thrum, you're in no condition. As soon as I get Miss Larimer and her aunt into town, and see to you, I'll get on the trail."

McIntyre shook his head. He was still staring at his son. "I'm goin', too. Soon as that fire's out, I'll form a posse. Get Casey back, send that whole pack to hell on a greasy platter." He paused, sighed. "Put somethin' over him, will you, Custis? Hate to see him layin' out there, so exposed."

"Sure thing, Thrum."

Longarm went inside the dress shop and came out with a length of dark muslin. He draped it over the young,

dead lawmen, and then looked at the burning bank and
the men scurrying around it like bees in a swarm. Just
then, the roof caved in, and the flames grew, shooting
out the top opening.

Longarm turned to his old friend. "I'm going to fetch
the two women I accompanied here from Denver, Thrum.
Then I'll help those men get that fire out. You stay there,
all right? Don't go movin' around too much. You don't
look well."

Thrum McIntyre leaned back against the awning support post, flanked by the dead, eyeless killer, and merely
shook his head as he stared at his dead son lying sprawled
in the street.

Longarm started walking back in the direction from
which he'd come. As he did, he pulled out a handkerchief and mopped his brow and mustache. The sun
burned down on him, still intense in early September.
He was sweating under his frock coat, but he hardly
noticed.

He was still trying to work through all that had happened in such a short time. He dreaded informing Cynthia, but when he reached the carriage, he saw no reason
to sugarcoat it. He could tell by the dark looks in both
Cynthia's and her aunt's eyes that the women were
expecting bad news.

And they got it.

Both sat back in the carriage's rear seat, flabbergasted,
while Longarm climbed into the driver's seat and hoorawed the smart-stepping Hanoverian back onto the trail
and into the town. Most of the men were fighting the fire,
so the dead men remained in the street, the dog that had
been barking now sniffing around one of the bodies.

Longarm stopped the carriage near where McIntyre still sat, looking sallow and jaundiced.

As he helped Cynthia down from the buggy, Longarm glanced at McIntyre and said, "Don't let him join that bucket brigade. He's had one heart attack, and he looks like he could have another one."

"I won't," Cynthia said, shaking her head. Her eyes were wide with disbelief as she looked at the dead men on the street and on the boardwalk around her. "Don't worry—Aunt Beatrice and I will see to Mr. McIntyre, Custis."

"I'm sorry about Casey," Longarm said. "But I'll get her back."

Cynthia's eyes filled with tears, but she put on as brave a face as possible and nodded.

"I'll be back soon," Longarm told her, and then helped Mrs. Schimpelfinnig down from the buggy, the old woman looking around and shaking her head with incredulity.

"Oh, good Lord," she kept saying half under her breath. "Oh, good Lord—when will men quit behaving like barbarians?"

As Cynthia and Mrs. Schimpelfinnig went over to be with McIntyre, Longarm removed his frock coat, rolled up his shirtsleeves, and joined the effort to douse the fire. He soon discovered that, as he'd expected, about all that could be done was to keep the fire from spreading.

Two hours later, he and the other townsmen had managed to do just that.

The bank was a smoldering hulk, with occasional flames still leaping from the windows, but the fire was contained. The buildings around it were doused and men were posted on all sides of the bank to make sure that no cinders sparked another fire.

Longarm walked back to where he'd left the carriage though the carriage and the Hanoverian were gone. The bodies had been carried out of the street, as well. An old black man was sitting on a loafer's bench out front of the Silver Spur Saloon, on the opposite side of the street from the ladies' dress shop, near where Thrum McIntyre had been shooting from.

The old black man had one blind white eye. He wore a straw hat, a time-worn chambray shirt, and suspenders. "I took the ladies' carriage—and some carriage it is, too—over to my livery barn on Wyoming Street yonder. Right across the street from the hotel the ladies got 'em a room at. Said to tell you where they was when you got done fightin' the fire, Mr. Lawman Suh."

Longarm walked over to the old-timer. "Name's Long. Custis Long, deputy U.S. marshal."

"Yes, sir, I heard you was comin'. I'm Wendell Calhoun." He shook his head, whistling under his breath. "That was some fine shootin'. Wish you woulda got here a little earlier. Sheriff McIntyre was a good lawdog in his time, but, just like the best of us, he done got old."

Longarm set one boot on the boardwalk near Calhoun and looked sadly over his shoulder at where McIntyre's son had lain. "I'm sorry I didn't get here sooner, too."

"Wouldn't have done the boy no good. He was dead as soon as them jaspers come runnin' out of the bank. Just happened to be walkin' by with his pretty girl." Calhoun shook his head and adjusted his dentures. "Shore is sad. 'Bout the saddest thing I ever seen since the war."

"You know how the sheriff is, Mr. Calhoun?"

"Feelin' poorly I'd say. I seen the doc headin' for his suite in the Arapaho—the same hotel them ladies is roomin' at. Doc's prob'ly with him now. The doc was out at the Leaf Ranch all night, deliverin' a newborn. One dies, another's born. Ain't that how it is?"

"I reckon."

"I hope you can save the girl, but I ain't holdin' out much hope. That Drummond bunch—they're jaspers of the first water. Low-down, dirty scum is what they is. Now that Colt is out of the pen, I just figured hell was gonna pop!"

"Well, you were right, Mr. Calhoun. Now, it's time for me to have a shot of whiskey and hit the trail. Where did you say that hotel was?"

Calhoun pointed east with the stem of a corncob pipe he held in his hand. "One block that way. You'll see the sign for Wyoming Street. Just south on that. Hotel's on the left, my barn's on the right."

"Much obliged."

Longarm started walking east along the street.

"You need a tracker, Marshal Long?"

Longarm stopped. The black man studied him wide-eyed, eager. "I was General Custer's best tracker up until the time o' the Washita . . ." The black man gave a sour look then dipped his chin resolutely. "You let me know if you could use the best tracker in Wyomin' Territory scoutin' them killers' trail."

"I'll do that, Mr. Calhoun." Longarm pinched his hat brim to the man.

"Call me Wendell."

"Longarm!" the federal badge toter returned as he jogged east along the street.

The hotel couldn't have been missed by a blind donkey. It was a large, three-story, green-and-pink Victorian with a sprawling, white wraparound porch with several rocking chairs. Longarm had heard that Arapaho was growing, and that more wealthy ranchers were moving herds into Platte County from Texas and Oklahoma. If the hotel was any indication of prosperity, he'd heard right.

Intending to check on the women as well as McIntyre, Longarm took the broad porch steps three at a time. He stopped on the porch as Mrs. Schimpelfinnig came out, cheeks flushed crimson, eyes wide as saucers. Her big picture hat was nearly hanging down one side of her head, causing what appeared a landslide of hair, pins, and small barrettes.

"Marshal!" the old woman intoned. "Cynthia!"

Longarm's heart thudded. "What about her?"

"She rented a horse from the livery barn and rode off after Miss Summerville and those . . . those . . . *kidnapping savages!*"

Chapter 6

Longarm's jaw hung to his chest as he gaped at Aunt Beatrice. *"Huh?"*

"She said she was going to pick up their trail and wait for you! Oh, the silly girl! I ordered her not to! I begged her! I pleaded! I am her aunt and her chaperone, after all!" Mrs. Schimpelfinnig stomped a foot and shook a fist in frustration. "I said, 'Cynthia, you must listen to me!' She merely kissed my cheek and ran off in her riding clothes. I even saw her dropping a pistol—*a pistol!*—into her satchel!"

"Where's my gear?" Longarm meant his rifle and saddlebags. He hadn't brought his McClellan saddle, which he usually hauled with him wherever he went, because he hadn't been expecting to ride in anything but the Larimer carriage.

Pressing a hand to her chest and staring south along the side street, Mrs. Schimpelfinnig said in a thin, quaking voice, "Cynthia secured a room for you. We had your gear stowed in there. Room nineteen, I believe. The key's at the front desk."

"Christ!" Longarm brushed past the woman and into the lobby.

He quickly picked up his key at the front desk, pausing to inquire with the elegant clerk in a black suit and foulard tie about the sheriff's condition. The man only shrugged and said the doctor was tending McIntyre in the sheriff's room.

Longarm cursed under his breath and ran up to his room. His mind was swirling. He couldn't believe that Cynthia had ridden off after that passel of cutthroats led by the notorious killer and bank robber Colt Drummond. But then, knowing Cynthia and how headstrong she was and how worried she'd been about her friend, Casey Summerville, the realization that Mrs. Schimpelfinnig hadn't been spouting gibberish hit Longarm like a rock to the forehead.

She said she'd wait when she'd picked up their trail. Longarm had a hard time believing that Cynthia could wait for anything. Once she got on the killers' trail, she was liable to keep riding until she'd ridden right up on them.

Or suppose Drummond had held some men back along the trail to wipe out a possible posse? Cynthia, like her friend Casey, would fall right smack-dab into Drummond's hands!

Longarm dug into one of his saddlebag pouches and took a pull from his bottle of Tom Moore Maryland Rye, calming himself down a little to figure out a plan. Like Cynthia, he'd have to rent a horse from the barn across the road. He opened his old nickeled railroad turnip. The

Ingersoll announced it was nearly four o'clock. He had
about two hours of good light left, which meant he had
to run Cynthia down as fast as possible.

He took another pull from the bottle of rye, then
corked it and returned it to his saddlebags. From the
opposite pouch, he withdrew his canteen and filled it
from the pitcher on the well-appointed room's washstand.
He donned his frock coat, slung the canteen over his
shoulder, picked up his rifle and saddlebags, and headed
back downstairs to the broad, dim lobby.

Mrs. Schimpelfennig was pacing the lobby like a
horse at the head of an approaching storm, holding a lacy
white handkerchief up close to her mouth to catch her
sniffs and sobs.

"Marshal Long, you will find her, won't you?" she
said, rushing over to Longarm and grabbing his arm.

"Of course I'll find her, Mrs. Schimpelfinnig. You go
on upstairs and lie down." Longarm paused near the front
door to pat the woman's hand and offer a weak smile.
"Try to take a little nap and then eat something. You're
way too distraught, ma'am. I hope to be back by sundown
or just a little later. Don't worry, now!"

That last he tossed back over his shoulder as he hurried out the door and down the porch steps. He sprinted
across the street to the barn and rented a stout, blaze-
faced sorrel with a white-speckled hindquarters from
Wendell Calhoun's grandson, Andy, who said that "the
well-setup white lady with purty black hair" rented a
steeldust stallion from him about fifty minutes earlier.

"The fastest horse of our whole cavvy!" the boy intoned, grinning.

He assured Longarm that the sorrel was the

second-fastest horse in the barn. Longarm saddled the
horse himself while the young man bridled him. Longarm strapped his rifle scabbard to the saddle, tossed the
saddlebags behind the cantle, and swung up into the
leather.

"That your wife, mister?" the boy wanted to know as
Longarm rammed his heels into the horse's flanks.

Longarm ignored the question. As he galloped past
the hotel and the three or four shanties planted willy-nilly
on this side of Arapaho, the boy called behind him, "She
shore is purty!"

Longarm followed a southern trail on out of town,
angling gradually toward the southwest and the steep,
brooding peaks of the Never Summer Mountains and the
Mummy Range as well as the Laramie Mountains and
several other ranges out that way. Cynthia must have
learned from someone, maybe the stable boy, where the
gang had headed with Casey Summerville in tow.

The trail followed what Longarm assumed to be Elk
Creek into a low jog of brown, piñon-stippled hills. The
creek curved off to the east, but the trail continued southwest through open, high-desert country relieved by the
low swells of hogbacks and stony dikes and cone-shaped
bluffs.

It was a vast country out here, with rugged peaks
looming distantly in all directions. This south-central
country of Wyoming Territory always made Longarm
feel small and insignificant, and he felt especially vul-
nerable now—on the trail of twenty men with one female
hostage, known rapists who would find two female hos-
tages even better.

Longarm had to catch up to Cynthia before she caught

up to Drummond. He knew Drummond's reputation as a merciless rapist as well as robber and cold-blooded killer. He'd get Cynthia safely back to town, and then go after the gang on a fresh horse in the morning and try like hell to get Casey Summerville out of the gang's depraved clutches.

Longarm pushed the sorrel as hard as he dared for nearly a half hour. Because he knew he wouldn't get anywhere by blowing the horse out or causing it to throw a shoe, he then stopped and rested the mount for ten minutes. When he'd watered it at a small run-out spring, he mounted up and continued along the trail for another mile before checking the mount down abruptly.

He stared at the trail beneath the horse's prancing hooves, bile filling his belly.

Longarm swung down from the saddle and, holding the sorrel's reins in one hand, he scoured the trail with his gaze. He could see the fresh tracks of what he assumed to be Cynthia's mount. They overlaid the tracks of many riders—those of Colt Drummond's bunch. But here he also saw three more tracks entering the trail and obscuring Cynthia's.

Longarm walked up the trail a little farther, following the jumbled tracks. Then he saw men's boot prints. They overlaid several prints of a smaller pair of boots—woman-sized, oval-toe, low-heeled boots.

Cynthia's riding boots.

Around her tracks and the men's tracks were many scuffles, detailing a skirmish. About ten yards farther on, the boot prints disappeared. There were only the relatively fresh tracks of four horses moving fast.

Longarm's heart hammered. The tracks told him the

story. Drummond had indeed left men behind to watch the gang's back trail and to likely scour it of a possible posse riding after them. But instead of a posse, the three men had spied a beautiful, black-haired woman riding toward them, and they'd overtaken her on the trail.

Longarm kicked a rock and stood with his boots spread in the middle of the trail, fists on his hips. He stared southwest, where the trail grew narrower and narrower as it meandered across the ever-darkening buttes.

They had her.

They had both Casey *and* Cynthia.

Longarm kicked another rock. "Damn fool girl!"

As he swung onto the sorrel's back, he looked around. The sun had nearly dropped behind the western peaks of the Wind River Range. Soon, it would be nearly as dark as the inside of a glove out here.

He had no choice. He had to go on.

He touched heels to the sorrel's flanks, loped on up the trail. He rode for another hour, then another. The sun sank amidst a painter's palette of vivid colors that slowly faded to a long line of bloodred. The sky grew a darker and darker green until the red disappeared and the dark sky was sprinkled with shimmering stars.

It had been good dark for an hour, and he was riding through the middle of a valley maybe a mile wide and bordered by tall bluffs, when he saw a pinprick of orange light ahead and to his right. The light flashed irregularly.

Longarm's blood quickened. What he was looking at, he knew from experience, was the light of a fire.

The flashing was caused by the breeze jostling branches between him and the blaze.

Quickly, Longarm reined the sorrel off the side of the trail, dismounted, and tied the horse to an aspen branch. He shucked his Winchester from the saddle boot, racked a round into the action, off cocked the hammer, and began walking slowly in the direction of the fire.

He meandered around trees, small shrubs, and rocks. He could hear the chuckling of a small creek off to his right, running along the base of the northern buttes. The breeze stirred the leaf-heavy branches of the aspens. A pinecone fell with a muffled thud.

Off in the far hills, a couple of coyotes were holding a woeful conversation.

As Longarm continued walking, setting each foot down carefully, unconsciously gritting his teeth in barely contained fury, the orange light grew steadily larger and brighter.

Finally, as he hunkered down behind a rock, he could see the flames dancing in a small clearing. The light reflected off the pine boughs angling over the bivouac. Three man-shaped figures were moving around the fire. It was a fairly large blaze, long flames dancing brightly, sending sparks skyward on columns of gray smoke.

Squeezing his rifle in his gloved hands, Longarm looked around, scowling. He couldn't see Cynthia. Had he been wrong about the girl being taken?

One of the men stumbled drunkenly to the right of the fire. He crouched over a shadow on the ground.

Longarm tipped his head, squinting.

No, not a shadow. It was a person the man was crouched over on the ground.

Pulse quickening in his temples, Longarm looked at the other two men sitting on separate logs around the fire.

They were holding cups in their hands. They had their heads turned toward the man hunkered over the fire on the ground.

The hunkered man was speaking loudly, but his back faced Longarm so the lawman couldn't hear what he was saying. The other two men were chuckling devilishly. He could see the orange firelight reflecting off their sweaty faces in the crevices of which dark shadows pooled.

Longarm rose from behind the rock and moved closer to the fire. He walked slowly, holding his rifle high across his chest. When he was about fifty yards away from the clearing, he dropped behind a log and doffed his hat.

He hunkered low, belly to the ground. He wanted to get a good handle on the layout before he took action. One careless or hasty move on his part could very easily get Cynthia killed.

He was nearly straight out from the figure on the ground. It was, indeed, Cynthia. The man who'd been hunkered over her was sitting on a rock on the other side of her, staring down at her. He had two pistols in his hands. From what he could see by the dancing light of the fire, Longarm thought they were cocked.

He could also see that Cynthia had been stripped naked. Her clothes were strewn between her and the creek. She was staked spread-eagle on the ground, her wrists and ankles tied to the stakes.

She was writhing and moaning, straining against her ties. Her full breasts shone golden in the firelight. They jostled as she struggled. She tossed her head, and her thick, inky black hair buffeted about her narrow shoulders.

The man nearest Cynthia rose drunkenly from the

rock he'd been sitting on. The firelight revealed that he wasn't wearing any pants. No underpants, either. Below the waist, he wore only white socks.

His erect dong jutted from between his shirttails.

Longarm drew a slow, hard breath through his nostrils and squeezed the rifle in his hands as though he were wringing the naked man's neck.

Chapter 7

"That there, my friends," said the half-naked man loudly, standing over Cynthia and slurring his words, aiming his cocked pistols down at the naked girl sprawled before him, "is the best hunk o' female flesh I do believe I ever laid eyes on."

"She shore ain't bad," agreed one of the men near the fire. One had his back to Longarm. The other faced him. But both men were understandably looking toward Cynthia.

The one with his back to Longarm said, "If you're gonna take her, Leon, then for chrissakes, take her, or I'm gonna come over there and take her myself!"

"You can kiss my ass, Jake!" said Leon, jerking his angry face toward the two at the fire. "We drew straws and I won, and I'm takin' her first . . . in my own sweet time. Me—I never had me a woman this fine-lookin', and—"

"And you probably never will again!" This from the man facing Longarm, who then tossed back whatever he had in his tin cup. Longarm had a feeling it wasn't coffee. All three men were good and drunk.

That was good in that they probably couldn't shoot as straight drunk as they could sober. But it was bad in that drunk men were more unpredictable than sober ones. And the very fact that they probably couldn't shoot straight could very well get Cynthia shot if it came to shooting, which it doubtless would.

There were also the possible ricochets to worry about.

Longarm wanted nothing more than to plant a bead on each of these sons o' bitches in turn and blow them to hell, but he admonished himself to move carefully, slowly.

"Ah, shut the hell up, George. You're getting' sloppy thirds!" Leon laughed and then dropped to his knees beside Cynthia. He stared down at her like a dog staring at a meaty bone.

Cynthia stared back at him. Her face was shielded by a thick wing of black hair. Her belly and breasts rose and fell sharply as she breathed. By the orange light, Longarm could see that her skin was slick and shiny with perspiration.

The poor girl had never faced anything like this before in her whole, moneyed life.

Longarm stared at the two pistols in Leon's hands. Leon held them down near Cynthia, aimed at her side. Longarm couldn't be absolutely sure that the guns were cocked, but if they were, they'd fire at the least bit of pressure. He had to wait until those pistols were aimed away from the girl before he started shooting.

"You sure are purty, honey," Leon said, shaking his head slowly. "Nice. Real nice."

"Let me go, you goatish bastard!" Cynthia spat at him. "Don't you have any self-respect at all? Is this the only way you can get a woman into your life—by stripping her naked and tying her up and taking her by *force*?"

By the fire, Jake laughed. "She got some gravel in her, that one. Purty and feisty. I like that!"

Leon chuckled, showing his teeth between his lips. He set one of his pistols on Cynthia's rising and falling belly. Longarm started to raise the Winchester he was squeezing in his hands, but he lowered the gun to the ground again when Leon raised the other pistol—the one in his left hand—and touched the barrel to Cynthia's nose.

He chuckled loudly enough that Longarm could hear him. Even hear him breathing through his nose. The man with the jutting hard-on slid the pistol very slowly down to her lips. He trailed the barrel down over her chin and down her neck. He slid it between her breasts that continued to rise and fall sharply as she breathed.

The man lifted the gun handle and raked the barrel up and down between her breasts, chuckling. The others chuckled, too, watching from the fire.

Flames of raw fury burned in Longarm's belly. He squeezed the Winchester, struggled with the urge to raise the rifle and begin shooting.

He could see clearly now that the pistol that the man was raking across Cynthia's naked body was, indeed, cocked. The slightest pressure on the trigger would cause the hammer to smash onto the cartridge, detonating it, most likely plunging the slug into the girl's sumptuous flesh.

Longarm had to wait until the man aimed the gun away from the lovely heiress. Even for a second. Then there would be some blood flying around here . . .

The man flicked the side of the gun barrel across Cynthia's left nipple, causing the breast to jiggle. He and the other men chuckled louder. The men by the fire were shifting around lustily. One reached down to adjust his crotch.

The man near Cynthia slid the gun barrel down the girl's belly.

"You son of a bitch," Longarm whispered, upper lip raised from his teeth, silently snarling.

The man slid the gun into the dark nest between Cynthia's spread legs. He poked the barrel inside her. Longarm could see the pink folds open.

Cynthia writhed, groaned. She arched her back, bent her knees, fought against her stays to no avail.

The man shoved the gun barrel in and out of her slowly, sneering down at her, showing his teeth. As he continued moving the pistol in and out of her, he lowered his head to her bosom and raked his nose up and down her deep cleavage.

"You bastard," Cynthia cried, breathless. "Oh, you bastard!"

The men by the fire had fallen silent now. Their heads were turned toward Cynthia and the other men. Their shoulders rose and fell slowly. One sighed heavily, shook his head, brushed a fist across his nose, and continued staring at the man fucking Cynthia with the cocked pistol.

Finally, the half-naked man raised the revolver.

Longarm steeled himself, watching intently, his right thumb caressing the Winchester's cocked hammer.

The man aimed the pistol at Cynthia's head as he shoved his pelvis and jutting cock toward her mouth.

"You suck that," he growled. "You suck that, you little bitch."

Cynthia shook her head vehemently from side to side.

The man rammed the pistol against her left breast.

"You suck it!"

Cynthia lifted her head, turned it toward the man's jutting member. As she let the man slide the shaft between her lips, Longarm swallowed. His mouth went dry. He shifted his gaze from Cynthia's head to the pistol the man pressed against her breast.

Longarm's heartbeat quickened as the man slackened his gun hand. The pistol began to slide down off Cynthia's chest.

The man groaned.

The other two men rose from their logs near the fire and turned toward their partner and Cynthia. They were silent, dark-eyed, staring.

The gun slid down off Cynthia's chest, the barrel now aimed at the ground. Just as Longarm was beginning to rise from behind his covering log, the man near Cynthia let out a loud, shrill wail.

"Oh, you bitch!" he screamed, jerking the gun up.

Before he could get the gun raised to Cynthia's head, Longarm snapped his Winchester to his shoulder, planted a quick bead on the man's chest, and fired.

The man stumbled backward, howling, dropping his revolver and falling flat on his back, quivering and clamping both hands over his crotch.

The other two men shouted and jerked toward Longarm, dropping their cups with tinny thuds. One grabbed for the pistols on his hips while the other reached for a

Colt's revolver rifle leaning against the log on which he'd been sitting.

Longarm's Winchester crashed, spitting smoke and orange flames.

The would-be rapist with the pistols dropped both weapons in the dust as one slug tore through his sternum, causing his shirt to billow, while a second slug punched into his left cheekbone. He spun around and dropped to both knees beside an aspen, as though in prayer.

The other man had spun around as he grabbed his Colt revolving rifle and spun around again as he raised the rifle in his hands, sort of crouching over it and yelling, his face a mask of rage. He triggered one shot toward Longarm, who'd sidestepped to his left, and the slug went whistling off into the night before plunking into a tree.

Longarm fired three more rounds, triggering and levering the leaping, roaring Winchester, until the man with the Colt's rifle had tumbled off into the darkness beyond the fire, howling like a gut-shot lobo.

The man's screams were short-lived, as were those of the other two. As silence moved in over the clearing, Longarm lowered the Winchester and ran over to Cynthia, who lay staring up at him, her mouth open, eyes glazed in shock. Longarm set his rifle down and knelt beside the girl, ripping his folding barlow knife from the front right pocket of his tweed trousers.

"Good Christ, girl!"

"Custis."

"I'll have you free in just a second!"

As he leaned over her to cut through the rope tying her left wrist to the stake embedded in the ground, she said, slightly louder, "Custis, wait."

He stopped, hovering over her. He looked down at her. She stared up at him. Her mouth was open, and she was breathing slowly, heavily. Her eyes looked strange. Darker than usual. Deeper than usual. There was silent pleading in them.

"Don't," she said from deep in her throat.

Longarm bored his gaze into hers. He lowered his eyes to her parted lips. They trailed down to her breasts. The orbs rose and fell more and more sharply, the nipples distended.

Longarm felt a heaviness in his pants, a fire in his loins. He slid his gaze down past her expanding and contracting belly to the tuft of black hair between her spread thighs. It glistened in the orange light of the fire's dancing flames.

Longarm raised his gaze to hers. Her eyes were subtly, desperately pleading.

She swallowed.

"No," he said weakly.

She stared up at him with that deep, dark urgency. She slid her gaze to his swollen crotch, and her eyes widened, her jaws hardening.

Longarm stood, kicked out of his boots and gun rig, and shucked out of his clothes, tossing them carelessly aside. His heart hammered. His blood stormed through his veins. Cynthia stared at his swollen, jutting cock as he hunkered down between her spread knees.

She laughed almost savagely as he took his hand and slid the head of his cock against her sopping pussy.

"Oh, Christ!" she groaned, lifting her chin, the cords standing out in her neck. "Fuck me," she whispered, looking down at his cock slowly sliding into her. "Fuck me, Custis. *Fuck me!*"

He shoved forward off his knees, pushing his throbbing hard-on deep inside her. He dropped his body over hers, squeezed her breasts in his hands, and closed his mouth over her lips as he started to slide in and out of her. When he lifted his head, continuing to thrust himself against her, she licked his lips and chin like a truckling dog, whimpering deep in her chest.

"Fuck me!" she pleaded, straining against the stays that held her fast to the ground. "Oh, God . . . that feels so . . . wonderful!"

Longarm felt his own blood rise as he toiled away between her legs.

In and out.

In and out.

He varied his rhythm occasionally, pumping savagely, then more tenderly, pausing now and then to lick her breasts and kiss her lips and nuzzle her neck.

After he'd fucked her for ten minutes he pulled out altogether and endured the nasty look she gave him, her cobalt blues brushed with the salmon light of the fire dancing behind him.

He laughed and squeezed her breasts. She mewled and fought against the stays, causing the leather and the wood to creak, cursing him to continue.

He straightened his back, sat back against his heels, and using his pelvis, shoved the swollen mushroom head into her pink, black-tufted folds once more. He slid only the head in and out for a time. Cynthia tipped her head back, tensing all her limbs, and groaning like a lovesick she-wolf.

She flexed each knee in turn, wagged her head from side to side, her hair flying across her face and hiding her eyes.

"Oh, Custis . . . please . . . !" she begged, dropping her chin to stare down at their joined crotches. "Shove it in . . . all the *wayyy!*"

Longarm chuckled, sucked a deep breath, and then he rammed his shaft into her once more. Closing his hands over her hips, he pulled her against him while he rammed his own hips forward, thrusting in and out of her with gradually more speed.

Suddenly, he felt her womb grabbing him like a small, warm, wet hand. She groaned more passionately, turning her head wildly from side to side, causing the sticks and the leather to creak and sigh.

When Longarm could tell it was time, he leaned forward, hoisting himself up on his arms and his toes, and hammered them both on over the edge of the steep precipice they'd been teetering on, into oblivion.

He felt her womb spasming against him, coating him with hot honey that oozed out from between both their bodies to bathe his balls and his thighs.

Gradually, he stopped thrusting. He slowly lowered himself onto her and shoved his face between her sweat-bathed breasts.

From nearby came a soft thud.

Cynthia lifted her head to peer at something over Longarm's left shoulder. The fire blazed in her eyes as she screamed.

Chapter 8

Longarm wheeled, grabbed his Colt from its holster, and twisted around, clicking the hammer back. Two round eyes reflected the fire's umber light from just beyond the fire, near where one of Cynthia's three attackers lay. Above the eyes, large ears twitched.

Longarm eased the tension on the Colt's trigger and lowered the piece. "Horse." He sighed. "Just a horse, Cynthia."

"Oh, God," Cynthia said with a sigh, resting her head back against the ground.

The three dead men must have hobbled their horses and one had come to investigate the commotion. Now it shook its head and backed away, out of the sphere of shimmering firelight.

Longarm holstered his Colt, picked up the barlow knife where he'd dropped it, and cut the ropes binding Cynthia to the four stakes. When she was free, she sat up and threw her arms around him, burying her face in his bare chest.

"I'm sorry, Custis. I guess I acted a little impetuously when I rode out here. I just couldn't stop thinking about Casey."

"You never should have come out here, girl. Damn foolhardy."

"I just wanted to pick up their trail, so they couldn't get away. I knew you had your hands full with the fire . . ."

Longarm drew her more tightly against him and kissed her forehead. He pressed her badly mussed hair back from her face and looked at her. "You all right?"

She nodded. "I think I'll go wash in the creek."

"Me, too. Then we'd best pack up, camp a little farther upstream. The rest of the gang might have heard the shooting, might come to investigate. We don't need to be taking on twenty men alone in the dark."

Cynthia nodded. Longarm rose, took her hand, and together they walked over to where the creek bubbled over rocks. They both knelt and cupped water to their faces and their privates, washing themselves.

Longarm was aware of Cynthia casting occasional, furtive glances at him. He cast his own at her, sheepish and also incredulous about what had just occurred between them.

Love bred by violence.

He chalked it up to their anxiety, then took a long drink of the cool water, and returned to the camp and dressed. When Cynthia had also dressed, Longarm kicked dirt on the near-dead fire, retrieved his horse from where he'd left it downstream, and then saddled Cynthia's horse. He confiscated two of the dead men's bedrolls and some coffee, jerky, and biscuits they had in their saddlebags, freed their horses, and gave Cynthia a hand up onto her steeldust's back.

They rode upstream about a thousand yards, at a narrow spot in the canyon, and set up camp in a small horseshoe of the creek, in a nest of rocks and junipers. Longarm did not build a fire. The light would only attract those of Drummond's gang sent to investigate the shooting.

He and Cynthia unsaddled their horses and spread their bedrolls in the soft grass, in the lee of their saddles. She sat down on her blankets, leaned back against her saddle, and drew her knees up. She wore a long, green wool riding skirt and high-topped brown boots. She smoothed the dress down against her legs. The temperature had dropped down to the low fifties or so. Thin tendrils of vapor trailed around their heads as they breathed.

"What those men were doing to me," she said in a thin, pensive voice, staring off toward a powder-horn moon climbing over a black ridge, "is probably what the rest of the gang is doing to Casey."

"Don't think about it."

"Over and over." Cynthia shuddered.

"I'll get after them in the morning, do everything I can to get her away from them coyotes."

Cynthia looked at him. "*We* will. I'm going with you."

"No."

Longarm had dug his bottle out of his saddlebags. He popped the cork and handed the bottle down to her.

She took the bottle. "Custis, I'm—"

"No," he said, putting steel in his voice. "Take a drink of that. It'll warm you up and help you sleep."

Cynthia tipped the bottle back. She didn't take a very large sip before pulling the bottle back down. She made a face as she swallowed, then ran the back of her hand across her mouth. "I don't see how you drink that stuff."

She'd always been more of a port drinker.

"It's not going to help me sleep." She handed the bottle back to Longarm. "I won't be able to sleep, knowing that Casey's with those . . . men. Going through what she's going through and knowing that Ryan is dead. I wouldn't doubt it at all if she simply gave up, knowing that even if she does get away from those killers, she has nothing to go home to but heartbreak."

Longarm took a long pull from the bottle. He looked around, pricking his ears. Hearing nothing more than the horses breathing where they were tethered nearby, he took another pull from the bottle and then sat down beside Cynthia. He wrapped an arm around her, squeezed her reassuringly.

"I know it'll be hard, but try to get some sleep. It's late. Mornin' will be here before we know it."

She sighed and squirmed against him, wrapping both her arms around his waist and burying her face in his chest. She gave a sob, and then he felt her slump against him as her exhaustion overtook her.

Soon he could tell from the lack of tension in her body, and her slow, regular breaths, that she was asleep.

He leaned back against his saddle, holding her. A few

times he dozed, but mostly he sort of half lay there against his saddle, holding her, watching and listening, thinking about how he was going to run down twenty men and pry a girl out of their viselike grip.

If Casey was even still alive by the time he found her, that was. Men like those in Drummond's bunch would likely use her and cast her away like an old newspaper. Longarm knew that it was entirely likely that he'd find Casey Summerville lying dead in a ravine somewhere along the trail to the Never Summer range.

He looked down at Cynthia slumped against him, her eyes lightly closed, lips parted as she breathed in a deep, dreamless sleep. At least that hadn't happened to Cynthia. He'd never given much thought to love before, but he figured that to have been as fearful as he'd been for the heiress's fate, love must have found him, after all.

At the first pale brush of the false dawn, Longarm slipped out from beneath the beautiful, sleeping girl and gentled her back against his saddle. Quietly, he scoured the brush for deadfall. He'd build a fire and make some coffee with the supplies he'd confiscated from one of the three men he'd killed.

He could risk a fire now, with day coming on. Drummond's bunch was most likely headed south toward the Colorado border and the maze of mountains beyond. They'd hole up amongst those rugged peaks and wait for their trail to grow cold before heading on out of Colorado, spending their loot all along the way.

Then they hit another bank or a train, maybe a stage, take another girl or two . . .

Longarm built a fire, filled a pot at the creek, and set coffee to boil.

Dawn became a pale lamp gradually glowing brighter around him, and birds began chirping in the trees. He sat on a rock near his small, crackling fire, a cup of hot, black Arbuckles in his hand, and watched Cynthia sleep, one cheek pressed against the palm of an open hand.

The girl stirred, lifted her head with a start.

"Easy, girl," Longarm said. "All's well."

She blinked. When her frightened eyes found him, they softened, and she smiled. "That coffee smells good."

"Damn good. And just what the doctor ordered. I'll pour you a cup."

Cynthia stretched, rose, winced, and pressed a hand to her back. "Stiff," she said. "I can't imagine how you sleep on the cold, hard ground as often as you do, Custis."

"You get used to the creaks. No choice but to, I reckon."

As Longarm filled a second cup, Cynthia came over with a blanket draped around her shoulders. She hugged Longarm from behind, kissed his ear and his cheek. "I'm gonna go freshen up. Be right back."

He watched her walk away, her round rump swaying enticingly behind the tight, slitted riding skirt that offered a teasing glimpse of one long, pale leg. Her long, black hair hung free down her back to nearly her waist. The stygian tresses were prettily mussed and tangled, lending the refined young heiress an ever-so-vaguely savage air.

Longarm remembered the mad rutting of the night

before, her three attackers lying freshly dead around them. A vague guilt prodded him when his member stirred.

Cynthia returned to the camp, and they had a cup of coffee together and chewed biscuits and jerky. When the golden sun was beginning to poke above the eastern horizon, sending buttery spears across the sky, they saddled their horses. Longarm slid his rifle into his saddle scabbard and then walked over to where Cynthia was adjusting her left stirrup.

Knowing their parting was imminent, and that there was no way he was going to let her ride along with him on the trail of her kidnapped friend, Cynthia looked frustrated. Longarm wrapped an arm around her waist, kissed her cheek. "You head straight back to Arapaho, now, girl. Your aunt is probably beside herself."

"I want to ride with you in the worst way, Custis. Casey needs me." She turned to face him. "But I know when you've made up your mind."

"Don't let me catch you on my back trail," he said, pointing an admonishing finger at her.

"You won't," Cynthia said, nodding. "I promise. I'll ride straight back to Arapaho and wait."

Longarm engulfed the girl in his arms and squeezed her.

"I just hope you find her alive, Custis," Cynthia said.

"Me, too."

Longarm helped her into her saddle and watched her ride off along the creek, heading northeast. He watched until she was out of sight, and then he climbed into his own saddle and reined the horse through the woods and onto the trail that angled southwest, toward the Colorado border.

The tracks of many shod horses were still clear in the chalky dirt, with the occasional, relatively fresh horse apple. Longarm followed them, pushing the sorrel as fast as he dared, knowing that being set afoot out here in this wide open country, with ranches spread as wide as an old coyote's teeth, would mean that he'd likely lose the gang as well as any chance of saving Casey Summerville, and he'd have a long walk back to Arapaho.

The trail he followed through the morning forked in a couple of places, but it was not hard to see which tine the gang had taken. They continued heading southwest, toward the rugged, spruce-green peaks jutting on the southern horizon.

All he'd learned from the outlaw whom McIntyre had executed was that the gang was headed for a ranch cabin along Purgatory Creek in the Never Summers. Longarm knew that Purgatory Creek was a long, meandering creek that virtually split the Never Summers in two. Those mountains, barely distinguishable from several other ranges around them, were wild, savage country.

If he lost the gang's tracks, he'd have one bear of a time finding that ranch. There was a good chance that he never would.

Around eleven thirty, hearing something, Longarm reined the sorrel to a halt and turned the mount sideways. He stared off down his back trail.

He heard the sound again—the intermittent drumming of shod hooves. He squinted as he stared toward the north and eventually saw a dust plume rising between two sandstone dikes. From this distance of nearly a mile, he could make out a thumbnail-sized gob of brown pulling that dust plume along at a rapid clip.

Several riders heading toward him.

Apprehension tickled the back of the lawman's neck. Had Drummond's bunch circled around and picked up his trail? Were they now dogging *him*?

Chapter 9

Quickly, Longarm reined the sorrel off the side of the trace and into some thick scrub behind a butte that became a rocky crag halfway from its bottom. Longarm tied the grulla to a juniper branch, slid his Winchester from its scabbard, and jogged to the crag. He began climbing the badly eroded slope, boots slipping in the loose dirt and gravel.

Watching for rattlesnakes, he wended his way through the rocks until he was about fifteen feet from the top of the formation. He found a niche amongst the boulders overlooking the trail, dropped to a knee, levered a cartridge into the Winchester's action, and hunkered low, waiting.

From his position on the butte's shoulder, he could see about a quarter mile up trail. Gradually, the thudding of the galloping horses grew louder. He could feel the vibration through the rocks. He started to hear the animals snorting and blowing, the creak of saddle leather, and the rattle of bridle chains.

The gang appeared through the scrub, tracing a bend in the trail. Longarm raised his rifle, rested the barrel on a rock in front of him, and dipped his cheek to the stock, narrowing one eye as he aimed down the barrel.

The gang came around the bend, and Longarm instantly slackened his trigger finger. Thrum McIntyre was at the head of the pack that appeared to number around ten men. A chunk of tin flashed on the man's brown leather vest.

Longarm stepped out to one side, planting a boot on the edge of a rock and waving his Winchester broadly, ready to throw himself back into the niche if one of the posse members threw a hasty slug his way.

McIntyre turned his head toward Longarm. The old lawman's eyes widened beneath the brim of his brown, high-crowned Stetson. He started to reach for the rifle sheathed under his right thigh, but then he blinked in recognition and threw up his left hand, hauling back on his reins with the right one.

"Whoa! Stand down, boys!"

When the posse came to a dusty halt on the trail at the butte's base, Longarm shouldered his Winchester and said, "Thrum, what in the hell are you doin' out here?"

McIntyre held his jittery buckskin under tight rein, jerking in the saddle as the horse fidgeted, shook its head. "What the hell you mean, Custis? That passel of savages murdered my boy. I'm not dead, so I'm ridin' after 'em. Any sign of 'em yet?"

"I shot three that had waylaid Miss Larimer."

"Oh, no," McIntyre said, wincing. "Her aunt told

me the young lady had ridden after the gang. Did they kill her?"

Longarm scowled down the slope at the posse ensconced in billowing dust. He could smell the sweat of the lathered horses. "No, they didn't kill her. Didn't you meet her on the trail? I put her on her horse early this morning and headed her back toward Arapaho."

McIntyre scowled back at the federal lawman. "Hell, no—I haven't seen her. Hope she didn't get off the main trail, get herself lost."

Longarm cursed as he turned away and hiked back down the slope, weaving his way amongst the rocks. He scowled down at the ground, his rifle on his shoulder, as he leaped rocks and occasional clumps of dry, twisted buckbrush. Again he found himself worried about Cynthia.

There was only one route back to Arapaho. If she'd been on it, she would have met the posse somewhere along the trail. Since McIntyre hadn't seen the girl, she must have gotten off the trail—either intentionally or unintentionally.

Either way was bad. But, as much as he wanted to, Longarm didn't have time to try to track her down. He had to get after Drummond.

He tramped back to his horse and swung into the leather. He rode back out to the trail where McIntyre sat with the rest of the posse. There were eleven men— shopkeepers, by the look of them. Most wore shabby dress shirts and pants, their coats tied around their bed-rolls. While they were well-armed, the bulk of the weapons Longarm saw were old as dirt.

The oldest gent, in a three-piece suit and derby hat

and riding a mule, was armed with what appeared to be an old Civil War–model Leech & Rigdon—a Confederate-made cap-and-ball revolver that sported as much rust on its steel frame as bluing. Three inches of the barrel poked out the open-toed leather holster that the older gent wore on his thigh.

McIntyre read Longarm's mind. The old lawman glanced at the men behind him. "They'll do."

Longarm nodded, trying to conceal his wariness. Ten shopkeepers and one aging sheriff with a heart condition were no match for the Drummond gang. But it wasn't Longarm's place to turn them back.

Longarm pointed his sorrel up the trail and touched heels to the mount's flanks. McIntyre did the same, his buckskin matching the sorrel's stride to Longarm's left.

As they rode, Longarm looked his old friend over. Thrum rode stiff-backed, his jaws set hard, his eyes dark with a steely determination. The rage and grief fairly emanated from the old lawman. His face was just as pale and haggard as it had been yesterday, when McIntyre had been sitting on the boardwalk staring at his dead son. His shoulders appeared even more fragile, as though his long, thin arms could be pulled from their sockets with the least pressure.

Longarm wished his old friend had stayed in town with the rest of these men. But he understood why McIntyre and they had to be here, and he didn't blame them. Longarm just didn't think that his having these men behind him was going to up his odds much at running down Drummond's bunch. In fact, they mighty even hinder his efforts. Sometimes the silence and stealth of one man was as valuable a weapon as twelve armed men powdering a trail together.

All that day, McIntyre didn't say much. Neither did the others. During stops to water and feed and rest the horses, an uneasy, weary tension oozed from the group.

None aside from McIntyre and possibly the even older man with the shotgun and the mule wanted to be here. During a brief conversation while he and the others filled their canteens at a spring, Longarm learned that the old-timer was Milford Stanley, president of Arapaho Bank & Trust. Stanley and his wife had lived in the bank's second story while renting out the third story to a half dozen other citizens—all without homes now. One elderly lady, a widow, had died in the fire. The old banker was looking for a comeuppance as well to help out his old friend, McIntyre.

Longarm genuinely hoped he got that reckoning and didn't die bloody or suffer a stroke for his efforts.

They continued heading south through valleys that narrowed and then broadened. They followed canyons around mountain walls and climbed high into heavy conifer forests. Longarm could tell that the air was getting thinner, for he felt a dull ache in his head, and his horse seemed to be blowing harder, straining. The air was fresher, cooler.

A moon rose, allowing the posse to keep hammering the trail after dark. Longarm could tell by the tracks they were following, and by the horse apples that he occasionally tested with his fingers, that they were gaining on the gang. The farther they traveled from Arapaho, the more leisurely the gang's pace had become, as though they'd doubted they'd be followed beyond twenty miles or so.

The waxing moon was hovering high over the eastern ridges when Longarm reined the sorrel to a stop in a broad valley between pine-clad slopes. He held up a hand, and the others checked their own tired mounts down.

"What is it?" McIntyre said in a raspy voice. He coughed into his fist, spat to one side. The ride had been hard on the unhealthy man.

Longarm sniffed the air. "Smoke. There's a fire nearby." He glanced at the men flanking him. "Everyone, off the trail!"

He led the way off the trail's north side into a small grove of piñons and cedars studding several small knolls. The others followed and dismounted when he did—wearily, heavily, some of the men groaning, others sighing. The banker dropped his shotgun, which hit the ground with a clattering thud.

Longarm picked it up for the man, brushed it off, and handed it back to him.

"Thanks," Stanley said in a pinched voice. His old, potbellied body was worn out and stiff from the ride. In the moonlight, he looked miserable. "You think they're close?"

"Someone's close. That smoke's from a campfire. No point in ridin' right up on 'em."

Longarm slid his Winchester from his saddle boot. He plucked his field glasses from his saddlebags and looped the lanyard around his neck. He walked southeast, the direction from which the smell of the smoke had come.

The others tramped along behind him, stumbling, making more noise than they should have been. Someone kicked a rock and raked out a curse. McIntyre walked up alongside Longarm, holding his Winchester up high across his chest in both his gloved hands.

Longarm led the men up a low ridge. When he dropped to his hands and knees, the others did the same and crawled along behind him and McIntyre.

Near the crest, Longarm doffed his hat and edged a look over the ridge and into a canyon on the other side. Through the trees dropping away below him, he could see a flickering light. The milky blue moonlight shone on the roof of what appeared a low-slung cabin on the canyon floor, against a ridge and surrounded on three sides by evergreen forest. Smoke rose from the cabin's chimney, showing blue-gray in the moonlight.

Longarm raised his field glasses and studied the clearing in which the cabin sat. Flanking the cabin was what appeared a privy, a barn, a small building—possibly a springhouse—and at least two corrals. Dark, bulky shapes shifted around in one of the corrals.

"I do believe we've found 'em," Longarm said as he continued studying the canyon through the glasses.

McIntyre was gazing through his own spyglass. He was breathing hard and audibly, the air raking in and out of his tired lungs. Longarm could smell the sickly, vinegar-like sweat on the older man.

"Well, I'll be damned. Probably stopped to rest their horses for the last pull into the Never Summers."

"Why don't you and your men wait here while I check it out?" Longarm said. "We'd best be sure it's Drummond and not just some rancher's house."

"Their trail leads into that Canyon, Custis."

"Just the same, we'd best be sure."

McIntyre nodded. "All right. We'll all get a little closer."

He looked at the weary men spread out to his right and canted his head toward the canyon. Longarm wished that McIntyre would remain here on the ridge, but he was out of his jurisdiction. Hell, officially he wasn't even on duty. He was on vacation. McIntyre was calling the shots.

Longarm donned his hat with a sigh. He rose and walked up and over the ridge, staying as low as possible. He glanced to his right at the others stumbling over rocks and cursing under their breaths. Their weapons clattered. One man kept sniffling as though he'd picked up a chill.

Longarm shook his head as he made his way down the slope and into the pines. There appeared to be two tiers to the slope. The first tier was relatively short— maybe a hundred yards. The next one was shallower, and there was a mix of conifers as well as deciduous trees, mainly aspens and some wild mahogany and currant shrubs, growing on its slope.

Here, McIntyre and the others hunkered down with their weapons while Longarm continued down the last slope toward the canyon floor. From this slope, he could see the cabin more clearly. All of its windows appeared lit. The smoke continued to unfurl from the broad stone chimney on the cabin's far side.

Halfway down the second slope, Longarm stopped and dropped to a knee. He looked around carefully, using his ears as well as his nose in addition to his eyes. Drummond must have posted pickets around the perimeters of the yard—if it really was the Drummond gang holed up in the cabin, that was. To not post a guard would have been foolish, and Drummond hadn't lived long enough to gain the reputation he had by being foolish.

Savage, yes. Foolish, no.

But Longarm neither saw nor heard or smelled anything unnatural. The night was so quiet that he could occasionally hear the horses sniffing in the corral flanking the cabin and the yammer of a distant coyote and the hoot of an owl. But that was it.

And the near-total silence made him nervous.

He walked down another stretch of the slope. It was steep here so he sort of slid down sideways, holding his rifle in his left hand and holding his right one out toward the slope to catch himself if he fell. Something nudged his left shoulder.

He wheeled.

A pointed-toed, badly scuffed brown boot hung suspended before him. Longarm gave an involuntary shudder and stumbled backward. His left boot slipped, and he hit the ground on his ass.

He stared up at the brown boot that had nudged him. There were two boots hanging side by side. The toe of the left boot had been worn all the way through, showing a white sock. Longarm's gaze followed the boots up to a pair of denim-clad legs. Then he saw the entire figure of the man hanging from an aspen branch.

Another figure hung beside the first.

Longarm gained his feet, holding his rifle in both hands, his thumb raking the hammer back. He stared up at a dark-clad, old, gray-faced woman hanging beside the old, bib-bearded man. They'd both been hanged from the same aspen branch.

They were likely the couple from the cabin. The

Drummond bunch had shown just how savage they actually were. They'd hanged the old couple, probably as a warning to anyone following, and taken over the cabin.

Longarm returned his gaze to the well-lit shack spewing smoke into the moonlit sky. Apprehension raked him.

Quiet. It was just too damn quiet. Silent.

What was Drummond up to?

Chapter 10

Longarm continued on down the slope from the hanging dead couple.

He stopped and looked around again when he reached the bottom of the ridge, and then moved to his left, slowly tracing a broad circle around the cabin. He moved so slowly and purposefully, all his senses alive, that it took nearly a half hour to reach the rear of the small springhouse that sat nearly directly behind the shack.

He knelt beside the springhouse, holding his rifle down low by his side so that the bright, pearl moonlight would not reflect off the barrel.

He was only sixty or so yards from the cabin's rear wall and the split stove wood stacked nearly to the rafters against it. He was close enough that he should be able to hear voices from inside—even through the stout pine timbers that the place had been hewn from. But there was nothing but silence save for the snorts and rustling of the horses in the corral left of the cabin.

Chicken flesh had risen between the lawman's shoulders. Something wasn't right. He knew that he ought to hightail it out of the yard, return to the ridge, and lead the posse away from the canyon until daylight. But he knew that McIntyre wouldn't go for that. Besides, a strong, urgent curiosity held him here.

Slowly, he stood, holding his rifle down low by his right leg. Quickly, he moved out away from the springhouse, jogging and crouching, until he'd gained the cabin's rear wall. He shouldered against it, leaned an ear to the rough, weathered-gray timbers.

Still only silence.

There were no windows in the rear wall so he moved around to the cabin's right side. There were two windows in the north wall. He sidled up to the first one, doffed his hat, and slowly edged a look around the frame.

Over the window was a lacy, white curtain that distorted Longarm's view. Beyond lay a room lit by a single candle guttering in an airtight tin on a dresser. The candle cast eerie umber light and menacing shadows. Longarm could see the dresser, a washstand, a chair, and a bed directly across from the dresser.

There was something large and lumpy on the bed, cast in shadow. It could have been a person lying there, or it could have been gear. Longarm tried to make it out, but then gave up and continued forward to the other window.

The view through this window was unobstructed. It showed a comfortably appointed sitting area and kitchen, the kitchen taking up about a third of the space near the hearth on the cabin's far side. The sitting room was nearest Longarm, with several large braided rugs and rocking chairs.

A wooden box stuffed with yarn and knitting needles sat under a table near one of the rockers, both arms and backs of which were hand-carved from moose horns.

Nothing appeared out of place. There was no mess, no gear, no litter of whiskey bottles. Most puzzling of all, there were none of Drummond's men loitering about. The cabin appeared empty.

Longarm glanced to the back of the cabin, then to the front. He stared straight out toward where the ridge humped darkly in the north.

Still, there were only the occasional yaps of a coyote and the intermittent hoots of an owl.

He walked around to the front of the cabin. He pivoted on his hips, holding the rifle straight out from his waist now, his index finger drawn taut across the trigger. He crossed the porch, opened the screen door, then the inside door, and stepped slowly into the cabin.

He sidestepped, pressed his back to the front wall beside the open door so he wouldn't be shot from behind. The fire popped and crackled. There was no other movement. Longarm started forward, wincing when his left boot came down on a loose floor puncheon, causing it to squawk.

From somewhere down a hall just ahead rose a muffled grunt. Remembering the lump he'd seen on the bed, Longarm aimed his Winchester straight out from his right hip and moved across the cabin, between the kitchen and parlor areas. He entered the dimly lit hall, setting each boot down quietly.

There was a doorway on the left and one on the right. Curtains hung over each.

Another grunt sounded from behind the curtain on the left.

Longarm drew a deep breath and slid the curtain back with his rifle barrel. He peered into the dimly lit room, saw the long lump on the bed moved. It was someone breathing, concealed by the room's dense shadows.

Longarm paused, looked around carefully, making sure no one was stealing up on him, and then pushed through the curtain. He stepped over to the bed and saw the half-naked girl with thick, long, curly blond staring up at him.

She had a thin blanket thrown over part of her, but a good half of her was bare, part of one breast exposed. She was tied spread-eagle, each limb bound to a bedpost.

A neckerchief was tied over her mouth, gagging her. Her blue eyes peered up through the screen of her mussed hair, sharp with desperation. The girl—she had to be Casey Summerville—shook her head and fought against her stays as well as the gag, groaning.

Longarm leaned his rifle against the bed and dug into his pants pocket for his barlow knife. The girl grunted and groaned, straining with more vigor, pleading with her eyes. She seemed to want desperately to speak. Longarm left his knife in his pocket and pulled the gag down onto her chin.

She lifted her head and, staring over his shoulder at something behind him, screamed, *"Look out!"*

Longarm wheeled, instantly grabbing his .44. A man

had entered the room behind him and was holding a rifle shoulder high, butt forward, the man's dark eyes wide with cunning. He gritted his teeth in a savage snarl as he thrust the rifle toward Longarm's head.

The lawman jerked to one side just in time. The steel butt plate grazed his left cheek a quarter second before he rammed his double-action Colt into the man's gut and triggered it three times.

The shots were muffled by the man's body.

The man, wearing a long, tan duster and sun-bleached brown Stetson, stumbled loudly backward, groaning and clapping his hands to his burning shirt. His shoulders and the back of his head smashed against the back wall and he dropped down the wall to his butt.

He lay on the floor, legs outstretched, his shirt smoking and sizzling from Longarm's gun flames, and dropped his hands to both sides. His eyes stared stupidly at Longarm as he gave one last, troubled sigh and lay still.

Longarm had just turned back to the girl when a rifle crashed in the distance. He whipped his head up and turned toward the curtained doorway at the base of which a pool of the killer's blood was spreading.

Another rifle cracked. Then another.

Men screamed.

The screams echoed and got lost amongst the veritable fusillade that had broken out on the ridge north of the cabin.

The blood sang in Longarm's ears, and the notion dawned on him at the same time the girl screamed, *"It's a trap!"*

Longarm shoved his Colt into its holster, grabbed his

rifle, and yelled, "I'll be back for you!" as he ran through the curtained doorway.

He crossed the cabin in five strides and bounded out the door. He dropped to a knee behind an awning support post and aimed his rifle straight out from his shoulder, toward the ridge where he'd left McIntyre and the others.

Against the ridge's velvety darkness, guns flashed like fireflies. Men whooped and hollered wildly as the rifles and pistols coughed and belched, and other men screamed and groaned. There was the wild, staggering-running sounds of snapping brush and trilling spurs.

Trap . . .

Longarm leaped off the porch, hit the ground, and began sprinting straight north toward the ridge, angling just right of where he'd come down and entered the ranch yard.

To his left, a gun flashed. The slug plunked into the ground behind Longarm. He kept running hard, his rifle in his right hand, and sprinted into the trees at the edge of the yard.

The gun to his left flashed again. The shooter was up the slope but below where the battle was being waged—if you could call it a battle, Longarm absently thought.

More like a slaughter . . .

He dropped behind a tree bole, aimed his rifle out to the left side of the pine, and fired two quick rounds at an inky shadow jostling toward him. He ejected his spent shell casing, levered a fresh one into the magazine, and held fire. He could no longer see the jostling shadow. No point in wasting precious lead.

He took off running up the slope, angling in the

general direction of where the shooting was slowly dying, the gun flashes growing more and more intermittent. As he climbed his heart hammered. Cold sweat basted his shirt against his back.

Trap. It had been a goddamn trap. Drummond had done a good job of springing it.

Rage burned in the lawman's belly, his shoulders. As he ran up the slope, angling toward the scene of what had most certainly been a massacre, he squeezed his rifle until his right hand ached. When he'd climbed about three quarters to the top of the ridge, he paused, dropped to a knee beside a pine, and caught his breath.

Straight along the slope toward the west, where the guns had belched and flashed only a few minutes before, was only darkness. Men were talking loudly. Some were laughing. Beneath the talking and the laughing, Longarm could hear another, obviously wounded man groaning. Mewling like a gut-shot coyote.

Longarm hardened his jaws, ground his molars. He raised his rifle, felt his index finger draw back against the Winchester's trigger. The finger twitched with his desperate, nearly irresistible compulsion to begin shooting and to keep shooting until he'd popped all his caps.

But he couldn't shoot in that direction without risking the lives any of the posse that weren't already dead.

There were two sharp pistol cracks. Longarm saw the lapping flames about fifty, maybe sixty yards straight off along the slope. They appeared to angle toward the ground. After the second shot, the wounded man stopped groaning.

Longarm drew a sharp breath, lowered his rifle. His

mind swam. Likely, the rest of the posse was dead. He was one man against nearly twenty.

What next?

He thought about the girl, Casey. He should have taken her and tried to slip up and over the ridge to the horses, but his mind had been with the posse. There had been nothing he could do for them, however. And he'd done nothing for the girl. He'd left her tied to the bed.

There was no going back for her now.

He considered opening up on the killers whom he could hear thrashing around in the brush ahead of him, talking, snickering, spurs jangling.

He reconsidered. Getting himself killed wasn't going to do Casey any good. He had to try to stay alive long enough to pull her away from Drummond's bunch once and for all.

Footsteps grew louder. A man's voice said, ". . . Over here somewhere. You fellas fan out. We'll . . ."

The voice was drowned by the snapping of branches and brush.

Longarm scuttled back behind the pine, pressed his back to it. He held his Winchester straight up and down between his legs, squeezing the barrel just above the forestock with his right hand, thinking it over. If he could take out one, two, maybe three of the gang without getting himself greased, he'd have that fewer to kill later . . .

He knew he should scuttle on up the ridge, but he rankled at the idea of hightailing it without sending a couple more of these bastards to hell.

He waited.

There were soft, crunching foot thumps straight along the slope to the west. He could hear at least two more men moving around downslope from him, between him and the ranch yard.

His pulse quickened as he continued listening, hearing the killers moving closer, closer . . .

He doffed his hat, turned his head to the right, pressing his cheek up against the side of the pine. Sap stuck to his cheek. The tang was heavy in his nose. In the corner of his right eye he could see a hatted shadow moving toward him, silhouetted by the moonlight.

Breath vapor plumed around the man's head. He was walking toward Longarm, meandering amongst the trees, crouched over a carbine that he aimed straight out from his left hip.

Longarm looked downslope. Two more inky figures, partly revealed by the moonlight, were milling around amongst the pines. One man on the downslope kicked something and cursed sharply but quietly. Another man to his left laughed.

They were a cocky bunch—Longarm would give them that.

Anger was a flame burning just behind his heart. The prospect of whittling the gang down by at least three more caused his heart to skip a beat. He raised the Winchester, curled his index finger through the trigger guard. With his right thumb, he softly, slowly ratcheted the hammer back to full cock.

The three men were moving toward him. Their footsteps were much louder now. The one moving straight toward him along the shoulder of the slope was probably only about twenty, fifteen feet away.

Longarm gave him another five seconds and then twisted around the left side of the tree and aimed his rifle straight west. He'd been wrong. The man was only ten feet away—so close that Longarm could smell his sweat. The man stopped, grunted.

Longarm's rifle barked loudly, echoing.

The man screamed. As he flew straight back, he triggered his rifle at the ground.

At the same time, Longarm racked a fresh round and fired at one of the two figures on the downslope.

Another scream.

He fired again, left of his last shot.

"Oh, *fuck*!" cried the third man as his own rifle flashed orange. The slug tore into the tree bole inches above Longarm's head, causing slivers of bark to rain onto his head.

The third man had dropped to a knee and was struggling to cock his rifle.

Longarm quickly rose and fired three more quick rounds down the slope and watched with satisfaction through his own wafting gray powder smoke as the third shooter was thrown backward and went cartwheeling on down the slope and out of sight in the darkness.

A voice yelled from downslope. "Rainey, George— you fellas get him?"

Silence.

Longarm couldn't help but allow himself a savage grin.

"No, they didn't get me!" he shouted, listening to his own echo vault around the canyon. "But I'll be back to get the rest of you sons o' bitches! And when I do, there'll be hell to pay and no hot pitch!"

Longarm wheeled and quickly climbed the ridge, chuckling savagely.

Chapter 11

Longarm didn't think any of Drummond's men were coming for him. When he'd climbed to the top of the ridge, he paused and stared out over the canyon.

Nothing but silence. He could see the flickering lights of the cabin, and little else. The moon had risen higher, shifting shadows.

Longarm looked down the slope to the right, where he'd left McIntyre and the rest of the posse. Only silence from that direction, too. An eerie, ominous silence like that in a graveyard at midnight.

Longarm hated to leave the posse, but he had no choice. Drummond might figure on him returning for them. He'd likely have at least one, maybe two men picketed over the dead men. Longarm couldn't take the chance. He'd camp a ways away from the canyon for the rest of the night and return the next morning to see to both the posse and Drummond's bunch.

Weariness was heavy inside him as he made his way

back to where he and the others had tied their horses. He'd untied the sorrel and was about to step into the saddle when he stopped. He looked back toward the ridge.

He couldn't leave the posse without one more look and listen. One or two might still be alive . . .

He retied his horse and walked back up to the ridge. He dropped to a knee just below the crest, doffed his hat to make himself a smaller target, and waited, staring into the valley that was dark save for the lights of the cabin. He looked down the ridge into the trees. No movement. No sound. Nothing.

Drummond's bunch had most likely made sure they'd killed all of the posse members before heading back to the cabin.

Longarm leaned his rifle against his shoulder and raked a gloved hand through his close-cropped hair. He set his hat on his head and rose. He'd started back down the slope toward the horses when brush crunched and crackled behind him. There was a thump and a groan.

Longarm wheeled, quietly racking a round into the Winchester's breech and aiming straight down the dark slope from his right hip. He scowled into the darkness, waiting for a gun flash. None came.

Another groan. About thirty yards down the slope, at the edge of the pines, a shadow moved.

Longarm walked slowly, cautiously back up to the ridge crest and down the other side, keeping the rifle aimed from his hip. The shadow was a man writhing on the ground at the edge of the trees, groaning. Longarm quickened his pace. He knelt down beside the man, who lay belly down, trying feebly to rise to his hands and knees.

It was McIntyre. Longarm could see the man's thick, gray-blond hair and mustache, the lanky frame clad in dark trousers, cream shirt, and brown vest. Longarm grabbed his arm.

"Thrum!"

The man jerked his arm away with a start and lifted his fear-sharp eyes to Longarm. He blinked, relaxed. "Custis," he rasped.

"How bad you hit?"

McIntyre shook his head. In a pinched voice, he said, "Not as bad as the others."

With Longarm's help, the sheriff rose to his knees and sat back on his heels. There was a dark stain low on his right side. The moonlight glistened in it. "I . . . I went back to fetch . . . medicine from my . . . saddlebags. I'd just started back when I heard the shooting."

The old lawman wagged his head. His breath rattled in his throat. "I ran down to try to stop it—I figured it was a bushwhack. Drummond was holed up in the trees yonder—waitin' to dry gulch us. I went runnin' down through the trees, yellin' to warn the others. Several of Drummond's men fired on me though I don't think they ever saw me. When I took this here bullet, I hid amongst some rocks."

"Can you stand, Thrum?"

Breathing hard, McIntyre nodded. He gave Longarm his arm, and the federal lawman helped the man to his feet. The man's knees wobbled. Longarm wrapped an arm around McIntyre's waist and led him up and over the ridge, heading back in the direction of the horses.

"Goddamn, low-down, dirty, dry-gulchin' bastards!" McIntyre rasped. "They musta been waitin' in the trees,

snuck around behind us." He looked at Longarm, showing his teeth beneath his thick, gray soup-strainer mustache. "They just walked down there and executed those
men. Ten of my friends—all good businessmen—from
Arapaho! Just like they was shootin' sick cattle,
Custis!"

"Easy, Thrum. Don't talk. We gotta get you to a camp,
warm fire, see about tendin' that bullet hole."

"Fuck the bullet hole. They killed my boy! They just
killed ten of Arapaho's most prominent businessmen!"

"Nothin' we can do about it now, Thrum." They
were almost back to the horses shifting around in the
darkness, the mounts' eyes reflecting the moonlight.
"Later . . . after we get that hole tended."

Longarm helped McIntyre onto his buckskin and then
he untied the other horses so they could roam and forage.
Some area rancher would likely add them to his remuda.
Longarm swung up onto his sorrel's back and, leading
McIntyre's horse by its reins, rode back down the trail.

Some of the other horses followed as he cut off the
trail and headed nearly straight west, toward a sloping,
forested ridge. The shrubs and junipers around him were
silvered by moonlight, revealing a deer path, which he
followed to the edge of the trees and then up through
the trees toward a relatively flat, rock-rimmed shelf in
the ridge wall.

He decided the shelf would be a good place to camp,
as the fire he'd build to get McIntyre warm and to brew
coffee would be concealed by the heavy pine growth.

When he'd helped the old lawman out of his saddle
and had eased him onto the ground, he unsaddled the
horses, gathered wood, and built a fire. He gave his bottle

of rye to the sheriff and told him to take several good pulls. McIntyre did so, weakly, as he sagged back against a rock outcropping, cursing between breaths.

By the light of the fire, Longarm opened his friend's shirt and inspected the wound. The thumb-sized hole was oozing thick, red blood that looked black in the darkness tempered by the fire's low flames. The blood ran down the sheriff's side, staining his cartridge belt, holster, and pants.

"How's it look?" McIntyre asked, tipping his head back against the outcropping and stretching his lips away from his teeth. He shuddered as pain waves rolled through him.

"Ain't gonna sugarcoat it for you, Thrum. It don't look good."

"Don't feel good, neither."

Longarm gently leaned the man forward, lifted his bloody shirt up, and inspected his back. "The bullet appears to have gone all the way through. Hard to tell how much damage it did. Might've torn up your liver. About all I can do is clean it the wound, stuff something in it so you don't bleed dry, and wrap it."

When McIntyre didn't say anything, Longarm looked at the man. He was surprised to see his old friend smiling at him.

"Ah, fuck, Custis, it don't matter one way or the other. When I seen my boy lyin' there in the street yesterday, most of me died right then. A good chunk of me died when his ma passed on over the range three years ago. It was my boy, Ryan, who kept me goin'. I figured even after the heart seizure that I might live to see a grandchild or two, but now . . . ah, fuck it. If you can keep me alive

for a few hours, shit, all I really want to do is kill Drummond. Then I'll be on my way out of this old world. Truth
be told, it ain't really worth a shit, anyway"—he smiled
again, ironically—"is it?"

"It don't look like it—no," Longarm had to admit.

He hadn't seen so much cold-blooded murder in a long
time. The depredations of the Drummond gang might
have been the worst he'd ever seen. He thought of the girl
he'd left in the cabin and berated himself once more for
not getting her out when he'd had the chance.

He used water from his canteen and whiskey to clean
McIntyre's wound. He tore a clean handkerchief in two,
soaked both swatches in rye, and stuffed one into the
entrance hole, the other into the exit hole, and wrapped
a long bandage tightly around the old sheriff's waist.

McIntyre had an extra shirt in his saddlebags, and
Longarm helped him into it. When the sheriff was resting
relatively comfortably in his blankets, Longarm offered
him some jerky and coffee. McIntyre waved it off.

"Do believe I'll sleep now, Custis," McIntyre said.

Before Longarm had time to respond the man was
snoring beneath his hat.

Longarm finished off his jerky and sat sipping his
coffee, which he'd liberally laced with rye. He stared off
through the dark forest toward the canyon in which the
Drummond gang was residing for the evening.

While fatigue was an anvil on the federal lawman's
shoulders, he wished desperately for the sun to rise so he
could get back after the gang. He'd hunt them like a pro-
fessional wildcat hunter hunted mountain lions—so quietly and stealthily that his quarry wouldn't know it was
being hunted.

He'd try to isolate them and kill them off by ones and twos. And in that fashion, he'd slowly make his way to Casey Summerville . . . if she was still alive tomorrow or the next day, that was. Longarm didn't doubt that as soon as they tired of the girl's body, they'd kill her and dump her somewhere along the trail.

It was nearly false dawn before Longarm finally slept for an hour, maybe a little more. When he opened his eyes, the sun was poking its head above the eastern ridges.

He rose on his elbows, wincing at the stiffness in his bones, and looked at the fire. It had burned down to a mound of gray ashes. Birds chirped in the branches. Dew lay heavy in the grass and pine boughs.

Longarm looked over at McIntyre, who lay in the same position as when Longarm had last seen him. Only, the sheriff's chest was not rising and falling. In fact, he lay still as stone beneath his blankets, his face obscured by his tipped-down hat.

Longarm tossed his own blankets aside and crawled over to McIntyre. He nudged the man's arm. "Thrum?"

No response.

Longarm shook the man again, lifted his hat brim up off his forehead. McIntyre's lower jaw hung slack. His blue eyes stared up at Longarm, glassy in death.

Chapter 12

Longarm would have buried his old friend if he'd had the shovel and the time needed to dig a grave. As it was, he had neither. He knew that McIntyre wouldn't mind being left there by the cold ashes of the previous night's fire, wrapped in his blankets for his final sleep.

Relinquished to the bobcats and wolves and whatever other carrion-eaters wanted to clean his bones. What did it really matter if the worms and maggots got you under the sod or the coyotes and crows got you on top of it?

McIntyre would have wanted Longarm to get after Drummond as quickly as he could, to retrieve the young woman who would have been his daughter-in-law, and to see that as many of Drummond's gang as possible died hard.

Longarm saddled his sorrel and Thrum's buckskin. He'd take the second horse for Casey. If he managed to rescue the girl, she'd need a mount for the trip back to Arapaho.

Longarm gathered his gear and mounted up, then glanced at the blanket-wrapped bundle of Thrumond McIntyre, hat showing at the top, boots at the bottom. He tipped his hat brim to the man, said, "Have a good sleep, old friend," and rode off through the trees, trailing the buckskin by its bridle reins.

He dropped into the valley and the morning light that seemed far too bright for his mood.

He'd come to this country for a wedding. What he'd found instead was death piled atop death and bad men running like hydrophobic wolves with an innocent girl they'd likely abused every night since they'd taken her.

Longarm rode cautiously southeast to where he and the posse riders had tethered their horses the night before. He rode on past the place and carefully scouted the ridge before riding over it and into the trees. He looked around as he let the sorrel and buckskin pick their own way down the steep slope through the forest, angling toward where he'd remembered leaving McIntyre and the other men the night before.

The sorrel gave the first indication he was close. The horse stopped and nickered, shaking its head. It smelled death.

Longarm rode a little farther down the slope. And then he found them. Or what was left of them after the coyotes and possibly a bobcat had been on them, ripping and tearing. One of the men had been dragged a good ways from the others, his guts eaten out.

He found the banker lying in a bloody pile farther down the slope from the others. Stanley lay on his back, ankles crossed, as though he'd just laid down for a nap. Aside from the blood and the torn clothes, of course. And one pecked-out eye—likely by the magpie that had been sitting on his forehead until Longarm had ridden up.

The bird had winged up to light on a near branch, waiting.

Longarm dismounted, dropped the horses' reins, and slid his Winchester from his rifle boot. He walked down the hill to the edge of the forest. Shouldered up against a pine, he studied the ranch yard below.

No smoke rose from the stone chimney. Both corrals flanking the place were empty, gates yawning wide. The cabin's front door stood open. An eerie silence lay over the yard.

Drummond's bunch had apparently ridden on, as Longarm had suspected they would. Still, the outlaw leader might have left someone behind to scour him, Longarm, from their back trail, for they knew they'd left one man alive last night. He hoped they wouldn't suspect that only one man would follow a gang of their size, but he'd best assume they would and proceed with caution.

Mounting the sorrel and leading McIntyre's horse, he rode slowly down out of the trees and into the ranch yard, swinging his head from left to right and back again, wary of an ambush.

He carefully checked out the cabin and the outbuildings, and then, satisfied that all of Drummond's gang had ridden on, he followed their tracks out of the yard and onto a wagon trail running along a creek that flowed west through the canyon.

He put the sorrel into a jog but did not slide his rifle into its boot. He rode with a cartridge in the chamber, the hammer at half cock, the barrel resting across his saddlebow.

Ready.

He had to assume that Drummond would hold a couple of riders back to watch for shadowers, because that's what he'd done before, when they'd grabbed Cynthia.

Cynthia . . .

The beautiful heiress had been a perpetual concern in the back of Longarm's mind. He glanced behind once out of some vague sense that she might be back there somewhere, following him. He'd seen no sign of her, however, and he hoped like hell she'd returned to Arapaho.

The trail that Drummond's bunch was following curved east toward a little mining town. The gang did not head east, however. It continued along what appeared to be an old Indian hunting trail westward along the canyon and then up and over a steep ridge through thick evergreen forest.

They dropped into yet another canyon on the other side and picked up another trail, proceeding to the southwest, heading ever closer to the Never Summer range and their hideout canyon on Purgatory Creek.

Longarm thought that he and the gang had crossed the Wyoming border and were in Colorado Territory now, heading into the maze of mountains northeast of Longs Peak, whose flame-shaped crest he could occasionally glimpse between mountains.

The gang was moving fast, stopping their horses only once every ninety minutes or so and then only long enough to let the beasts draw water at creeks and eat a little grass. Judging by the sign, the men dismounted and smoked quirleys or cigars and in one case, a pipe— Longarm saw a cold dottle of gray ash in some brome-grass under a cottonwood—before riding on.

He kept a sharp eye out for the girl's body, knowing it was likely the gang would dispose of Miss Summerville at any time. The thought graveled him with dread. He wanted to be able to save at least one person from the gang. One more in addition to Cynthia. They'd done enough killing for one spree.

Drummond's outfit was a hard-to-predict bunch, however. By four o'clock that afternoon, Longarm had come upon no drag riders who'd attempted to bushwhack him, as he'd suspected they would. That led him to believe that they were cocky enough to believe that the one man they'd left alive on the ridge the night before would not be foolhardy enough to shadow them solo.

And that was just fine with Longarm. Maybe they were also cocky enough to let their guards down enough to allow him to sneak into their camp later that night, and try to pull Miss Summerville to safety . . .

After dusk, Longarm slowed his pace and rode with a keener sense of caution. Now would be a good time for Drummond to dry gulch him. And there was also the possibility he could ride right up onto their camp without knowing until he saw the flashes and heard the gunfire, and then it would be too late for him as well as the girl.

The sun had drifted all the way down and darkness had closed over the canyon while leaving a tinge of green in the sky, when Longarm heard voices and smelled wood smoke. Immediately, he reined his horses off the trail and into the forest, slipping quietly out of the saddle and tying both mounts to a branch.

"Stay, fellas," he said, patting the sorrel's wither.

He shouldered the rifle and walked up through the

trees. There was a gradual incline that led to a rocky ridge crest spiked with cedars and junipers.

The wind was blowing up here. It blew the smoke up toward Longarm, flavored with the smell of boiling coffee and roasting meat. Rabbit, Longarm thought, having eaten only jerky and canned peaches with water all day.

His mouth watered and his stomach ached at the smell.

He crouched amongst the rocks and stared down into the canyon on the other side of the ridge. The outlaws' camp was only a hundred yards down the slope. Longarm could see the flames bending and sparking in the wind, see shadows moving around them, hear the voices of the men speaking, occasionally laughing. Someone dropped a pan on a rock.

There was an ironlike clang and a curse before a shrill voice yelled, "Damn, that was hot!"

Another man said, "Well, what do you expect, Billy— it was on the fire, ya damn fool!"

Another man laughed.

The wind obscured the conversation for a time but between wind gusts, Longarm heard one man say, ". . . Ought to have the little bitch cookin' for us. I mean . . ."

Then another said with a chuckle, "Hell, she's too damn busy . . . !"

Another gust of wind and the ensuing cracking of a pine branch drowned the rest of the man's sentence.

Longarm was grateful for the wind. Its noise would cover any sounds he might make, and, since it was blowing out of the south, it would keep the gang's horses from scenting him.

He wasted no time in moving down out of the rocks

and into the trees, quartering left of the camp. He kept the fire a good hundred yards away on his right, picking his way carefully through the trees.

He'd find a place to hole up beyond the firelight, out of sight and hearing of the gang, and try to locate Casey.

When he had a good handle on her location, he'd wait for the gang to roll up in their blankets and to fall good asleep. Then he'd see if it was possible to sneak in and slip the girl out from under the outlaws' noses without getting himself and the girl killed.

When he'd stolen around amidst the dark columns of the creaking pines for about fifteen minutes, he stopped and dropped to a knee. The fire was about seventy yards away, ahead and on his right. He had a fair view of it through a natural aisle in the forest.

He could see the men sitting or lounging around, drinking and talking, occasionally reaching toward their steel-frame spit and pulling a chunk of meat from what appeared to be a deer they were roasting. He could hear the men talking but he couldn't hear them now amongst the creaking, blowing trees, beneath the steady sighing of the wind.

Longarm saw the fire reflected in the grease drifting off the spitted beast, see the smoke the dripping grease lifted when it hit the coals. He swallowed, aware of the stabbing hunger in his belly.

What he wouldn't give for a cup of coffee laced with rye and a good chunk of that meat . . .

He shook the thought aside and frowned as he scrutinized the men and the piled tack for Casey. No sign of the girl. One of the men had said she was "busy." What did that mean?

He knew what it meant.

He slipped out away from the tree, tracing a broad half circle around the camp. There were lots of shrubs and rocks amongst the pines, offering good cover. He wove his way around them as he continued circling the fire, looking for both Casey and the gang's horses that might wind him and give him away with a startled nicker.

Longarm was moving between two aspens when he glimpsed a shadow moving amongst the trees between him and the fire, which was about eighty yards away now, due to the course he'd followed between patches of cover. He stopped, dropped to a knee behind an aspen, doffed his hat and looked out around the tree.

There were two shadows milling around what appeared a few scattered, gray boulders between Longarm and the fire, about thirty yards ahead and on his left. He thought he saw the firelight glint off blond hair, and his pulse quickened.

He stepped away from the aspen, moving slowly to his left, crouching over his rifle to shield the light from the barrel and breech. He made his way toward the two shadows, and when he was about thirty yards away from them and could hear a man's voice as well as a woman's, he hunkered down behind a boulder.

They were ahead of him now, and slightly right. They stood in front of a low volcanic dike humping up darkly from the ground. The man was speaking in low tones. He was facing the girl, who cried out softly when he swung her away from him and threw her up against the escarpment.

"Goddamn you!" she said.

The man laughed and grabbed a handful of her hair

and leaned close to speak into her left ear. She wore a red-and-black checked shirt and denims that were too large for her—the pants of one of the gang members, no doubt. They must have ripped the clothes she'd started out with off of her.

Longarm looked around, saw a boulder nearer the man and Casey, and scuttled quietly over to it, staying so low that he was almost crawling. When he reached the boulder, he doffed his hat and kept his head down, squeezing his rifle in his hands.

He could hear the girl grunting. When he slid a cautious look around the edge of the boulder, he saw why.

The man had her bent forward against a boulder about the same size as the one covering Longarm. Her head bobbed and she clutched at the rock as the man thrust against her from behind.

He wore a black hat banded with hammered silver, a black shirt, and a red neckerchief. He was about Longarm's size, maybe a little shorter. Longarm thought he had a trimmed beard and mustache but it was hard to see much about him in the dark.

As the killer rammed his cock in and out of the girl, he grunted sharply and lifted his chin to suck air through his clenched teeth.

"Mighty fine!" he rasped, reaching forward to squeeze her breasts between the flaps of her open shirt. "Oh, yeah—you're mighty fine, Miss Casey. Woulda made that sheriff a right fine wife. You sure would!"

Two small fires of rage burned behind Longarm's eyes. He started to raise the rifle.

He'd shoot the son of a bitch before he finished, and then he'd cut loose on the camp and try to kill as many of the other gang members as he could before he swept the girl over his shoulder and carted her the hell out of here.

The gang would be so surprised by Longarm's ambush that they'd think twice or three times before following him and Casey in the dark.

Longarm rose to a crouch and pressed the Winchester's rear stock against his shoulder. He clicked the hammer back to full cock.

Casey laughed. At least, Longarm thought she'd laughed.

He eased the tension in his trigger finger, scowling at the two people entangled nearby.

The girl laughed again and groaned as she turned around, squirming, to face her tormentor.

"Hey, what you doin'?" asked the man who'd been raping her.

"I want to watch your big, handsome face while you fuck me," Casey said, leaning forward to kiss him. "Oh, Colt," she said, placing her hands on his bearded cheeks, rubbing her nose against his, "I can't wait until we're in Mexico together, lying on a warm beach—with all that money to spend!"

Longarm was glad his lower jaw was well attached to his face. If it hadn't been, he'd be picking it up out of the dirt at his boots about now.

Chapter 13

Longarm pulled his head back down behind the rock. A sick feeling threatened to overtake him. His head reeled.

Could he have actually heard what he thought he'd heard?

The girl's husky laughter was all the answer he needed, but then he also heard her say between grunts, "We'll be able to do this all the time . . . and much more comfortably . . . down in Mexico, Colt . . ."

Colt?

The man hammering away between her legs was none other than Colt Drummond himself.

Longarm tried to think through his options now as the two grunted and groaned together against the rock just beyond his own. But then he jerked with a start when a near pistol barked.

The shot was somewhat muffled but Longarm could still tell that it had come from nearby.

Even more flabbergasted than before, he lifted his

head above the boulder and stared toward Colt Drummond and Casey Summerville. Drummond was still crouched over the girl. But he'd stopped thrusting his hips. In the light of the moon just now rising, Longarm could see the whites of the outlaw's eyes as he stared down at the girl.

Gray smoke wafted between them.

Near the fire, someone yelled. Then someone else yelled. Colt Drummond jerked back away from Casey, shambling backward.

"Did you like that, Colt?" Casey said, straightening. Longarm saw the gun in her left hand. Then he saw the empty holster on Drummond's right hip.

"That was for Ryan, you slimy son of a bitch. Just one more thing before I let you die—Ryan knew how to please a woman, an art that you obviously have never learned."

"You bitch," Drummond said, standing wobbly-legged in front of Casey, wide-eyed in shock. The bloodstain on his shirt was growing. "You fuckin', double-crossin' whore!"

Casey cackled an evil laugh. "You're the whore, you son of a bitch." She raised the smoking gun, aiming at Drummond's chest.

"No!" the outlaw leader screamed, stumbling backward.

As he got his feet entangled in his pants and started to fall, Casey triggered the Colt once more at Drummond. The outlaw screamed as he twisted around and fell on his side.

Now the men from the direction of the fire were shouting and grabbing their gloves, some breaking into runs toward the spot of the gunfire. As Casey reached down to pull her pants up around her waist, Longarm stepped up beside her and said, "Don't shoot me, girl—I'm a friend of Cynthia Larimer's and I'm here to help!"

Casey gasped and stumbled away from him as he raised his rifle to his shoulder and began slinging lead toward the outlaws running toward him, their jouncing figures silhouetted by the orange light of the large fire behind them.

One man groaned. Another screamed. A couple more hit the ground before the others fanned out, diving for cover.

Casey stood to Longarm's left, staring at him in wide-eyed surprise, aiming her pistol at him but letting her arm sag. Her shirt was still open, her pants unbuttoned.

Longarm glanced at her and yelled, "Pull yourself together and get ready to run!"

When he'd fired two more shots, his Winchester's hammer pinged on an empty chamber. Casey had crouched down behind the boulder against which she and Drummond had been toiling. Longarm fired two shots with his Colt .44 and yelled, "Ready, Miss Summerville?"

"Yes!"

Longarm quickly emptied the pistol, holding the shouting outlaws at bay, and then holstered the weapon. He swung around and grabbed Casey's arm. "Run! Follow me!" He nearly tripped over a deadfall. "Watch your step!"

"Who did you say you were?" the girl called behind him, breathing hard as she ran.

"Custis P. Long, deputy U.S. marshal out of Denver."

"Oh, my gosh," Casey said with quiet astonishment. "Yes . . . Cynthia told me about you."

Despite the popping of pistols and the hollow crashes of rifles behind him, Longarm felt his ears warm a little in chagrin, wondering just how much Cynthia had told Casey about her and Longarm's relationship. He ran ducking around branches and swerving around trees. Casey followed close on his heels.

She stumbled over a fallen branch, and Longarm stopped and pulled her back to her feet. He gave her a tug, and they continued running back in the direction from which Longarm had come.

Behind them, gunfire crackled in the direction of the fire. Men were yelling and running hard, crunching brush beneath their boots. Longarm could hear their spurs jingling raucously beneath the wind.

At the edge of the trees, Longarm yelled, "Keep going. I'm going to make sure we're not followed!"

Breathing hard, Casey ran past him and started up the slope. Longarm stood facing in the direction from which they'd come, his back to a tree. Guns flashed and popped. Shadows jerked and swayed as the gang members ran through the brush.

"They shot Colt!" one of them shouted. "They gut-shot Colt—*get* them sons o' bitches, whoever in hell they are!"

Longarm watched the shadows and the gun flashes. Most of the shots were wild, as the gang members appeared to have lost Longarm's and Casey's trail. One, however, was running and leaping through the brush, heading toward Longarm.

About fifty feet away, the man stopped suddenly and stood facing Longarm. The federal lawman could see the man's shoulders rise and fall as he breathed, looking around and listening, trying to get some sense of where the gang's captive and rescuer and had gone. He couldn't see Longarm against the dark tree.

Up the slope behind Longarm, Casey gave a groan. There was a rattle of slide-rock and a thump. She must have fallen. The man facing Longarm heard her.

"This way!" he shouted, and continued running toward Longarm—an inky, hatted shadow against the firelight.

He hadn't taken two steps before Longarm leveled his Winchester on him and fired three times, the Winchester roaring in his hands. The man was about ten feet from Longarm when he gave a grunt and flew to one side, hitting the ground with a thud and a crunch of rustling brush.

Longarm turned slightly to his right and opened fire on the other jostling shadows. Someone yelped. Several shadows leaped for cover.

Longarm swung around the tree and began running up the slope. About halfway up, Casey had fallen to her knees. She was breathing hard, staring toward him, her blond hair visible in the darkness.

"I'm so tired," she said.

"We'll rest soon."

Longarm pulled her up and took her hand. Running, he half dragged the girl along behind him. When they reached the ridge, Longarm found his and McIntyre's horses. He quickly untied the mounts. Casey stood nearby, hands on her knees as she tried to get her breath. She'd been through a lot and was understandable fatigued.

"Here we go!" Longarm said, wrapping his arms around the girl's waist and lifting her up onto the back of the buckskin. As he did so, his hands slid up her belly, beneath her shirt, and he was aware of a momentary prodding in his loins when he felt the undersides of her warm breasts brush against his hands.

He berated himself for the feeling. The girl had been through hell and here he was getting a schoolboy's thrill out of feeling her tits. Christ . . .

"Can you follow me?" Longarm said.

"Where are we going?"

Longarm could hear the men yelling below the ridge though they'd stopped shooting for now.

"As far away from here as we can get," he told the girl, staring up at her.

"I think you'd better take the reins," she said, leaning forward and wrapping both her hands around her saddle horn. "I doubt I'd be able to keep up with you."

"All right."

Holding the girl's reins, he stepped up onto the sorrel's back and galloped away from the ridge.

"Hold on good and tight!" he called back to her. "If I'm going too fast for you, yell and I'll try to slow down!"

He rode harder than he should have in the darkness, endangering both horses as well as himself and Casey. But he wanted to get away from the gang as quickly as he could and get the girl to relative safety, a quiet camp.

He rode hard but not long. When he found what appeared a good place to bivouac up a narrow side canyon, west of the one in which Drummond's bunch was camped, he stopped and helped the girl out of her saddle. She was light in his arms.

He set her down before him, and she sagged toward him weakly. He grabbed her shoulders.

"How you holdin' up?" he asked her.

She shook her head, lifted her chin. He'd only vaguely noticed how beautiful she was when he'd seen her in the dim cabin. Now her cornflower blue eyes seared through him, caused his throat to constrict. Her gold-blond hair was thick and wavy.

He bent down, picked her up in his arms, and set her on a rock near a blowdown tree. They were relatively sheltered here from the wind, but he could hear it howling along the crests of the two stony ridges towering darkly over him.

He walked back to his horse, hauled out his rye bottle, and popped the cork. He held out the bottle.

"Take a drink of that," he said. "Put some warmth in your bones until I can build us a fire."

She took the bottle, staring up at him. The flaps of her shirt blew up, showing a glimpse of her pale belly in the moonlight angling into the canyon. "How much . . . did you see back there?"

"Don't worry," Longarm said. "You did what you had to do to stay alive. No one in their right mind would hold it against you."

She lifted the bottle and took a sip.

Longarm turned and walked over to the horses. He'd just unbuckled his sorrel's latigo strap, when she said, "I only . . . laid with Drummond. Just Drummond. He kept me off-limits to the others."

Longarm slipped the saddle from the sorrel's back, and set it over another blowdown angling across several boulders. He didn't like the way she was making him feel, talking like that. He didn't want those images in his head. "You don't have to explain anything to me, Casey."

She took another small sip from the bottle and then rested the bottle against her thigh. "I just feel . . . so dirty. I . . . *fucked* . . . the man who gunned my husband-to-be down in the main street of Arapaho. He raped me, and then I let him, and then I decided the only way to stay alive was to lay with him willingly."

"And then you shot him." Longarm winked at her. "That's A-one in my book. And young Ryan would be mighty proud of you, too."

"I still feel dirty. Just . . . so . . . awfully . . . *dirty!*"

He glanced to where a thin stream ran down the gently sloping floor of the narrow canyon. "Water over there. Help yourself." He removed a small cake of potash lye soap and a towel from his saddlebags, and handed both to her. "Go on over and wash. You'll feel better. By the time you're done, I'll have a fire built."

She accepted the towel and the soap, brushing a finger across his thumb. "Thank you, Deputy Long."

"Call me Longarm."

"All right." Casey offered a weak smile. "Longarm."

Casey's horse whinnied. The sorrel followed suit. Both horses tightened their muscles and arched their tails. Longarm grabbed his rifle, cocked it, and stared down canyon.

Now he could hear the clacks of horse hooves on the canyon's stony floor. He raised the rifle but eased the tension in his trigger finger. The single rider wasn't doing anything to conceal his approach.

Puzzling . . .

"Hello, the camp." A familiar voice. A *woman's* voice.

Longarm scowled as the shadow of the horse and rider slid into the moonlight. He saw the young woman's long, black hair blowing in the breeze.

"Cynthia?"

"Custis? Yes, it's me—don't shoot."

As she approached, Longarm leaned his rifle against a rock and strode out to meet her, grabbing her horse's bridle. "What in the hell are you doing here? I told you to—"

"Cynthia!" Casey said, walking out away from the rock she'd been sitting on.

"Oh, God, Casey!" Cynthia slipped lithely out of the saddle and ran over to engulf her friend in her arms. The two women hugged, rocking slowly together for a long time. Longarm watched them, holding the bridle of Cynthia's horse, scowling.

"Are you all right?" Cynthia asked, her voice muffled as the two women clung to each other.

Casey shook her head, grunted. She lifted her head and looked at Cynthia. "They killed Ryan."

"I know, my love," Cynthia said, sobbing. "I know. But you're going to be all right—aren't you?" She placed her hands on both sides of her friend's face. "Please tell me you are, Casey."

Casey nodded. "Yes, I'll be all right. In time." She glanced at Longarm. "But only because of your friend, Longarm."

Cynthia turned to the big lawman still staring in

frustration at her. "Yes, he is handy to have around, isn't he?"

"I was just about to wash in the stream," Casey said, holding up her towel and the small cake of soap. "Help me?"

"Sure."

Cynthia glanced obliquely over her shoulder at Longarm as she and her friend walked toward the dark line of the stream cutting down the middle of the canyon floor, at the base of the northern ridge. The water sparkled like diamonds in the moonlight.

Longarm gave a caustic chuff and began unsaddling Cynthia's horse.

Chapter 14

Longarm built a fire while the women bathed in the creek.

He could hear them talking quietly, hear the water splashing softly, as he gathered wood and started a small fire in a well-sheltered stone ring. A few times he heard Casey sob, but mostly the women talked, Cynthia consoling her friend, trying to quell the pain of all that she'd been through.

He had the fire burning well, the camp set up, and coffee brewing, when the women returned. They sat down on the blankets that Longarm had rolled out, and gathered other blankets around their shoulders, staving off the chill. Longarm glanced at Cynthia. She did not return the look; she seemed to be sheepishly trying to avoid meeting his gaze.

When the coffee was ready, Longarm poured them each a cup and added a liberal jigger of whiskey to each. He handed out the rest of the jerky, and they sat around the fire, nibbling the jerky and sipping the coffee. No one said anything. Casey stared sadly into the flames, as did Cynthia, who had one arm draped over her friend's shoulders.

Longarm took the time for only one cup of coffee. Then he grabbed his rifle and said, "I'm going to walk back down canyon a ways, see if we were followed."

"And if we were?" Cynthia said, looking at him now, her eyes wide.

"Then we're in trouble."

Longarm walked off, and he heard Cynthia say behind him, "He's angry with me."

Casey said something but Longarm couldn't make it out, because just then the wind howled over the top of the canyon. It dwindled enough that he could hear Cynthia say, "Yeah, I think so," in a wistful sort of way, looking toward him.

She thought what? he vaguely wondered as he continued walking down the canyon.

He didn't think about it long. There were too many more important things on his mind.

Carefully, he scouted the area around where the side canyon led off from the main one. Using a branch, he rubbed out his and the women's tracks where they led into the side canyon. A good tracker could still find them by the light of day, but it would be much harder now at night. He was glad he didn't smell the smoke from the fire he'd built.

After a half hour of sitting and watching the main canyon from a boulder nest, and concluding that Drummond's bunch wouldn't follow him until tomorrow, he headed back to the fire. Cynthia had added wood to it.

He found her lying against his own saddle while Casey slept curled on her side beneath her blankets on the fire's opposite side, facing the flames.

Cynthia had hers and his blankets pulled up to her chin.

Longarm stopped near the fire, and looked down at her. She looked up at him, glanced at Casey who appeared sound asleep on the other side of the crackling flames, and pressed two gloved fingers to her rich lips.

Longarm leaned his rifle against a rock, knelt beside her, and said quietly, "I oughta rip that skirt off of you and strap your naked ass for defying me like this."

She arched a brow. "We'd look silly if Casey woke up—now, wouldn't we?"

Longarm glanced at Casey. "I doubt an earthquake would wake the poor girl."

"She's my closest friend, Custis. I couldn't ride back to Arapaho and leave her out here."

"You been following me the whole time?"

"I lost you early yesterday until I heard the gunfire a while ago. You and Casey crossed the trail in front of me, and I followed."

"You're a sneaky one, Miss Larimer."

Cynthia shook her head and glanced at her friend sleeping on the other side of the fire. "I just couldn't leave her. I really thought you'd find her dead, however. Thank God you didn't."

"She'll be all right. She's a lot like you."

"How's that?"

"She's got sand. When I found her she'd just popped a couple of pills into Colt Drummond's belly."

Cynthia sighed and nodded as she looked toward Casey. "She told me all about it."

"Everything?"

Cynthia looked at Longarm. "Everything."

Longarm reached for the coffeepot. "Another cup?"

She shook her head. "Just the whiskey, if there's enough."

"There's enough," Longarm said, grabbing his bottle. "Thrum has a bottle in his saddlebags."

"Where is the sheriff?"

"Dead."

Cynthia sucked her cheeks in and looked down at her cup as Longarm poured whiskey into it. "So many killed. When will it stop?"

"When Drummond's bunch is all dead."

Cynthia sipped her whiskey and leaned her head on Longarm's shoulder. "You're not going after them alone, now, are you? There's no point now that we have Casey back."

"They're wolves with blood-washed fangs. If they're not stopped, they'll keep on killing. But I don't think I'm going to need to go after them."

She set her hand on his thigh, slid her cheek around on his shoulder. "How's that?"

"They'll be comin' after us. Matter of pride, if for no other reason."

"I had a feeling that's what you were going to say."

"We'll head on out of here at first wash of dawn. Travel the backcountry. If the gang starts to pull close, I'll send you and Casey ahead and try to lead them off your trail, set up a bushwhack somewhere."

Cynthia glanced at the starry sky. "We don't have much time, then."

"No." Longarm pulled her close and kissed her forehead. "You'd better get some sleep. I'm gonna stay awake, keep an eye and an ear skinned."

Cynthia slid her hand inside his thigh until her fingertips burned like lanterns against his crotch. "I had something else in mind."

"Gotta keep my head clear."

"Me, too." She smiled up at him as she unbuttoned his fly. "Won't take long. Just want to show my appreciation for saving my friend . . . as well as myself."

"Cynthia, Christ," he whispered, his heart thumping with desire as well as anxiety. He could feel her hands burning into his crotch as she finagled the buttons. He turned to gaze off down canyon, making sure an attack wasn't imminent.

He doubted that the gang would come tonight and risk getting themselves ambushed in the darkness for the trouble. If they did, Longarm was confident the horses would alert him, as they had to Cynthia's approach.

He sucked a breath when she reached through his open fly and into his balbriggans and wrapped a hand around his half-hard dong. She squirmed against him as she gently pulled it out of his pants and caressed it gently. It nodded its head, attentive to the girl's ministrations, and stood up straight and tall.

Longarm glanced across the fire toward where Casey lay on her side, nearly covered by Longarm's spare blanket. Her eyes glittered for just a second, and he canted his head and frowned over the shifting flames. He was sure that her eyes were closed now, but had they been open a second ago?

What else would have caused them to glitter like that?

"This ain't exactly . . . um . . . private," Longarm told Cynthia.

But then she lowered her head and dropped her hot mouth over the swollen head of his iron-hard organ, and he ceased to care about anything except for the playful proddings of the heiress's tongue.

"Christ," he grunted, leaning back against his saddle and extending his legs straight out in front of him.

Cynthia lifted her mouth from his cock and swallowed. "You like?"

"Jesus."

She placed one hand around the base of his organ and held it steady while she lapped it like a heifer on a salt block. Longarm glanced once more at Casey.

The girl appeared to be sleeping. He must have only imagined that her eyes had been open. Now, as Cynthia twirled her tongue around on the tip of his bulging head, he closed his eyes and ground his heels into the dirt in front of the fire ring.

Cynthia slid her mouth down on him until he could feel her tonsils expanding and contracting against the head of his swollen mast. She gave a little gag and then lifted her mouth. She lowered it again, lifted it, gradually increasing her pace until the warm tingling spread upward from his crotch and into his belly and chest.

His throat constricted.

He ground his heels deeper into the dirt, tipped his head far back until his hat tumbled onto his saddle, and he cut loose with a groan that he tried like hell to stifle.

His seed geysered up out of his cock and down the girl's throat. She kept sucking, choking, sucking, gagging until she couldn't swallow any more of it, and then she lifted her head and pumped him with both hands.

The pearl fluid continued to ooze up over the head and down onto her hands. It crackled as she massaged him, her hands gradually moving slower and slower until she finally withdrew them and touched a finger to her lip and sucked it.

"You taste good," she said.

Longarm opened his eyes. He frowned suspiciously when he caught that glitter of reflected light again on the other side of the fire. But when he studied Casey more closely, he saw that her eyes were closed.

He was so spent and sated that he no longer much cared.

Cynthia rose. "Shall we pay a little visit to the creek?" she asked.

Longarm swallowed the knot in his throat and caught his breath. He shoved his dwindling member back inside his pants and buttoned up. "Reckon we'd better," he said and rose.

When Cynthia had rolled up in her blankets beside Casey, Longarm added another small log to the fire, keeping the flames about the size of a small afternoon coffee fire, and picked up his rifle. He lifted the collar of his frock coat against the mountain chill and walked back down the canyon.

He hunkered down in a nest of some rocks at the intersection of the two canyons and kept watch for about an hour. The only movement was the fluttering of the leaves, sage, and grass in the occasional breeze, the infrequent flicking past of a hunting night bird, and the steady, gradual sliding of the stars across the firmament.

Unable to keep his eyes open any longer, he dozed, resting his head back against the rock behind him. Something woke him so that he was instantly awake, shoving his hat brim up off his forehead and looking around.

He could tell by the dimming of the stars that it was false dawn. Birds were singing and fluttering in the aspens on the other side of the main canyon to his left. Straight ahead of him, down the west canyon, there was the high clack of a shod hoof striking a stone.

Then he could hear the thuds of more horses heading toward him. He frowned, staring into the misty shadows between canyon walls. Silhouettes shifted, jostled, bounced as the riders—a whole pack of them—moved toward him.

The group kept coming until the shadows separated and became individual horses and riders. The men were not talking but were riding in grim silence, leaning out from their horses to scour the canyon floor with their eyes.

Longarm hunkered lower in his stone nest, resting his rifle across his thighs. Very slowly, gritting his teeth, he pumped a fresh cartridge into the chamber. He slid his head to the left, edging a look around the rock in front of him, and then it drew it back behind the rock.

The riders were within fifty yards and approaching at a fast walk. Longarm's heartbeat quickened.

If the gang discovered his trail leading into the side canyon, he'd have to open up on them. It was hard to tell in the morning shadows, but he thought there were ten or twelve of them. He'd thinned their ranks considerably the night before, killing a few and wounding others, but the gang was still of formidable size.

He couldn't get them all here—not with a nine-shot Winchester, a six-shot Colt revolver, and the two-shot derringer stuffed into a vest pocket and attached to his old Ingersoll by a gold-washed chain. But if they started up the side canyon in which the two women lay asleep, he'd have to give the gang all he had.

He listened to the loudening clacks and thuds of the horses. He heard the squawk of leather and the rattle of bridle chains and bits. A horse nickered softly.

Now he could smell the horses, hear one of the riders cough. Another grunted.

Then the gang was beside him, moving off behind him on his left. His heartbeat picked up its pace. If they'd seen the mouth of the side canyon, they were not heading into it!

He turned his head slightly left to see the group riding past his position—all holding rifles. One of the men at the front of the group said quietly, "How you holdin' up, Colt?"

Longarm beetled his brows. Colt? He'd thought that Casey's bullet would have sent the man to his reward . . .

"Doin' all right, Dusty," Colt Drummond said in a low, raspy voice. "Doin' all right. Bullet must have just skidded off a rib. The second one just burned my other side. I'll be all right."

"Be even better once we find the girl and the son of a bitch who helped her, eh, Boss?" asked one of the men riding behind Colt Drummond, who was one of the two lead riders.

"You got that right, Skinny," Drummond said, his

voice dwindling now with distance as the gang rode on up the canyon, hooves clacking and thudding. "When I see her again, she's gonna be a long time dyin'. A long time dyin', a long time *screamin'* . . ."

When they were out of sight, Longarm worked his way out of his nest of rocks and ran up the canyon. The fire was out, the young women still curled up in their blankets to one side of it.

Longarm reached down and grabbed the arms of each, and both gasped with starts as he said, "Sorry, ladies, but it's time to pull our picket pins."

"What's happened?" Casey said, sitting up and sliding her tangled blond hair from her eyes.

"Drummond's on the move," Longarm said, grabbing his saddle blanket and saddle and hauling both over to his horse picketed nearby.

"Drummond?" Casey was incredulous. "You mean Drummond's men."

"No, I mean Drummond. He's still kickin'. Prob'ly not so high, but he's kickin', just the same!"

"Damn!" Casey intoned, slamming her fists against her thighs. "I should have pumped one more bullet into that bastard's bread basket!"

"That's all right," Cynthia said, quickly gaining her feet and grabbing her boots. "We'll get him."

Longarm tossed his saddle blanket up over the sorrel's back. "We? I don't think . . ."

"Yes, we," Casey said, sitting down on the same rock as Cynthia, both women grunting softly as they pulled on their boots. "I want a hand in his killing. In the killing of all of them."

Longarm opened his mouth to protest, but she cut him

off with, "I appreciate your saving my life back there, Longarm. But you're not going to stop me from going after that bunch, same as you. Drummond and his cutthroats have taken too much away from me. The only thing I have left to lose is my life, and right now, without the man I love in it anymore, my life doesn't look like much at all."

Longarm glanced at Cynthia, who returned his look with a determined one of her own as she pulled on her second boot. The lawman merely shook his head and grunted as he continued saddling his horse.

When he was finished rigging the sorrel, he helped the women saddle their own mounts. He'd just helped Casey onto the back of McIntyre's buckskin when the sorrel jerked its head down canyon and whinnied sharply. Longarm turned to stare in the same direction as the horse.

In the gray morning shadows he saw a dark, manshaped figure sidled up to a large rock, aiming a rifle. "Down!" Longarm shouted, reaching for his Winchester.

Too late.

The bushwhacker's rifle crashed, stabbing flames toward the camp.

Cynthia had been tying her bedroll together by the cold fire ring. She screamed and flew forward over the bedroll, hitting the ground on her belly.

Chapter 15

"Cynthia!" Longarm and Casey shouted at the same time, a half second before the lawman dropped to a knee with his Winchester and triggered three quick shots.

His slugs blew the bushwhacker back away from the rock with a startled yelp, dropping his rifle and hitting the ground on his back.

"Cynthia!" Longarm ran over to where Cynthia lay sprawled belly down over her blanket roll.

"I'm all right," the girl said in a thin, startled voice, lifting her head. "It just grazed me."

Longarm saw the torn left shoulder seam of her leather jacket. No blood appeared. Cynthia shook her head. "Where did that come from?"

Longarm and Casey, who'd leaped out of her saddle and come running, pulled Cynthia to her feet.

"We got company," Longarm said, leading Cynthia to her steeldust and staring back at where the bushwhacker lay unmoving behind the boulder at the side of the trail leading up from the main canyon. "You two mount up and get moving. I'll be right behind you!"

"Custis, you come, too!" Cynthia yelled as he half flung and half hoisted her onto her steeldust.

"I'll be right behind you—now haul ass!" Longarm slapped the steeldust's hip, and the horse lurched into a gallop on up the side canyon. Casey ground her heels into her own horse's flanks and followed Cynthia around a bend and out of sight behind the curving stone wall.

Longarm ran down toward where the dead man lay. He held his rifle in one hand high, ready to fire if he needed to. He looked around cautiously but saw no other movement.

He dropped to a knee beside the dead man, who lay staring up at him, eyes dull. One of Longarm's shots had blown out his left temple. The other had taken him through a shoulder. Blood trickled out a corner of his mouth.

Longarm stared down canyon toward the main one and spied the shifting shadows of oncoming riders along the narrow, shadow-dense corridor. At the same time, he could hear the clacking of several sets of horse hooves on the canyon's stone floor.

"Shit," Longarm groused and picked up the dead man's Winchester. The man had an extra cartridge belt around his waist, the loops filled with .44 shells. Longarm quickly removed it, hung it over his shoulder, and ran back up the narrow canyon to his sorrel.

He shoved the spare rifle into his saddle boot, wrapped the extra cartridge belt around his own waist, and stepped into the leather. A second later he was galloping on up the gently rising floor of the cut, casting a quick glance over his left shoulder.

The riders just then galloped around a slight bulge in the wall and reined up in front of the dead man. Longarm spied four riders—inky silhouettes against the gray-brown morning shadows.

They spied him at the same time, one pointing and yelling, "There!"

Longarm pulled the sorrel around a bend in the canyon wall and kept riding, climbing the narrow trail and caressing the hammer of his Winchester with his thumb. Ten minutes later, he closed on the women riding ahead between the steep ridge walls.

Cynthia stopped her horse and turned toward him. He threw his left arm forward, shouting angrily, "Go! Keeping going! What the hell you stopping for?"

"Are they coming?" she yelled back at him.

"Of course they're coming!"

Having to worry about the two women—two headstrong beauties with revenge on their minds—had soured his mood. He felt as though he were herding a passel of young hellcats.

He and the women pushed on up the canyon. The sun was climbing above the horizon by the time they reached the top of the canyon pass, where the stone walls dropped away and a fragrant forest took over. Longarm led the way along a breezy ridge and then swung away from the ridge and up and over a higher pass.

Now the sun was well above the horizon and the day was heating up.

He checked the sorrel down and told the two girls to keep riding. He'd catch up to them.

He rose in his saddle to see over the crest of the pass he'd just crossed and into the valley on the other side.

The riders were just now making their way around an outcropping—four in all.

The gang must have split up, and these four had been the first to hear the scouting bushwhacker fire at Cynthia. The others had likely heard the shots, as well, and were a little farther behind.

Longarm wanted to rub these four off his trail and whittle the gang's total number down to a more manageable size.

He sat back down in his saddle and stared down the slope, in the direction the girls were riding. Below and about a hundred yards away, the game trail they were following appeared to run through a large outcropping of limestone and sandstone—probably an ancient volcanic bubble that was all that remained of a more massive dike. It was a jumble of stone dominoes tossed this way and that, studded with cedars, piñons, and juniper, with a trail splitting it down the middle.

Longarm batted his heels against the sorrel's ribs. He galloped on down the slope through sun-dappled pines smelling sharply of sap and caught up to the women just as they entered the outcropping, the stony walls rising on both sides of the trail.

"Are they still behind us?" Cynthia asked.

"Yup."

"What are we going to do about that?" Casey wanted to know, reining her horse to a stop and turning toward Longarm. Her pretty blue eyes were resolute, urgent, even savage. She had a beautiful mouth, the lips red, the top one slightly upturned. Her nose was fine and long, her jaws straight and hard.

Yes, she had gravel, this one. After all she'd been

through, all she could think about—maybe the only thing that kept her from thinking about what might have been had the Drummond bunch not ridden into Arapaho that day—was blood justice.

Longarm stared at her gravely. He turned to Cynthia, who owned a look similar to her friend's.

"All right," he said. "You want blood? I'll give you blood. Can either of you shoot a rifle?"

Cynthia slid McIntyre's carbine from the saddle boot beneath her right thigh. Coolly, she said, "I might have been born with a silver spoon in my mouth, Marshal Long, but my uncle gave me a little target practice now and then . . . when Aunt May wasn't looking."

Longarm looked at Casey. "What about you, young lady?"

"Ryan knew this country. That meant he knew that women as well as men should know how to handle a revolver and a rifle . . . if things come to that."

Longarm tossed her the rifle he'd taken from the dead man. "I reckon things have come to that."

"Yes, they certainly have," Casey said, gritting her pretty teeth as she racked a fresh cartridge into the action.

"This way," Longarm said, glancing over his shoulder as he gigged the sorrel up ahead of the women and down the corridor that was about forty yards wide, with tufts of wiry brown grass growing up along the edges. The trail appeared to be used mostly by game and wild horses, maybe the occasional mule-mounted prospector.

At the far end, the where the walls of rubble gradually lowered before disappearing altogether, Longarm reined off the trail's left side. He swung down and tied his horse in a small grove of aspens, behind some large rocks. The women followed suit and then he led them up into the rocks until all three were overlooking the trail.

"Keep your heads down until I give you the wave," Longarm said. "I'll be up there." He indicated a higher point on their right. "Take your time, pick out a rider, and blow the bastard's head off!"

"I like the sound of that," Casey said.

"Oh, I do, too," Cynthia said. "I do, too."

Longarm glanced at each woman incredulously.

Their eyes were hard, jaws determined. Their mussed, dusty hair blew around their face. Longarm was, indeed, riding with a pair of hellcats. The prettiest pair of hellcats he'd ever laid eyes on, but hellcats just the same . . .

He gave a wry chuckle, then scrambled up into the rocks above the women's location and hunkered down behind a tongue-shaped boulder.

He looked down the trail. The four riders were coming down the ridge, their horses lunging forward and digging their hooves into the slope for purchase, dust billowing around them. There was one lead rider, two riding abreast behind him, and one riding about thirty yards behind, a red neckerchief billowing around his neck.

The lead rider was looking at the ground, making sure he was still on Longarm's and the women's trail. They were probably trying to figure out why there were three sets of horse tracks instead of two.

Just stay distracted, Longarm thought, pressing his right shoulder up against the side of the boulder and staring into the canyon below him. *Just stay distracted . . .*

He did not risk another look at the oncoming riders.

He judged their distance by the thuds of their horses' hooves. He looked down the rocks on his left. The women were hunkered low, side by side, squinting up at Longarm. They were awaiting his signal.

The horse clomps were getting louder. The riders were almost directly below, following Longarm's and the women's tracks.

"Careful in here, fellas," one of them said. "Damn good place for a . . . *oof!*"

Longarm had signaled the women, and they'd quickly aimed and fired, blowing the lead rider off his horse before he'd been able to finish his sentence. Longarm watched the women patiently shooting, saw another man blown off his horse and getting his left boot caught in the stirrup. The horse dragged the man about ten yards before the boot slipped free, and the rider slid and rolled, bellowing.

The girls had aimed well with their first shots, but the next shots were wild. There were two riders left, and they were now swinging down from their saddles and bolting for cover.

Longarm planted a bead on one and drilled the man in his lower back as the gent flew over a boulder on the far side of the gap. Longarm triggered another round at the feet of the other gent, who stopped suddenly, dropped to a knee, and flung a rifle round back toward Longarm.

The slug smashed against Longarm's covering boulder, the shrill spang setting up a ringing in the lawman's ears. Longarm had pulled his head back behind the rock. A rifle to his left crashed.

"Got him!" Casey cried.

Longarm looked into the gap below to see the fourth man crouched forward in the trail, crossing his arms on his belly. His rifle lay in the trail at his forehead, which he was grinding painfully into the ground.

Longarm thew up his right arm. "Hold your fire, ladies."

He looked into the canyon.

All four men were down. The lead rider lay on his back nearly directly below Longarm, a bullet hole tattooing his forehead.

The man who'd been dragged was on his back and writhing in pain, clutching a hand to the right side of his neck.

The third man lay unmoving in the rocks while the last rider just now rolled onto his back, clutching his belly with one hand, pounding the other hand against the ground, and cursing loudly. Longarm decided to go down and take a look. He rose and was about to tell the women to stay put until he told them it was safe, but they were no longer hunkered down in the rocks.

They were both scrambling down through the boulders, heading for the trail!

Longarm ground his teeth. "You two get back here, goddamnit!"

Ignoring him, they both climbed down the rocks until they were standing in the trail. Longarm headed that way himself, wending his way amongst the boulders.

When a man screamed, Longarm leaped atop a boulder near the trail. Casey and Cynthia were standing over the man who'd been dragged by his horse and who was now cupping a hand to the side of his bloody neck.

"Put that rifle down, you little bitch!" the man shouted,

glaring up at the pair. "Put it down this instant, or so help me . . . !"

"So help me what?" asked Casey in a sweet little voice that made Longarm's oysters tighten and draw up into his scrotum.

She cocked a fresh round into her carbine's breech.

"Hey!" the wounded man shouted. "I'm wounded. You got no call!"

Casey said, "You're one of the men who shot Ryan."

Longarm sucked a sharp breath. He remained atop the boulder. He saw no reason to interfere in a private matter. He wasn't really a lawman here, anyway. Officially, he was on vacation. He would be obligated to write no reports on this matter.

"Ryan? Who the fuck's Ryan?"

"Ryan was going to be my husband. He was the sheriff in Arapaho. You shot him . . . along with a few others of your gang."

The wounded man had a broad, freckled face, big ears sticking out the side of his skull. He swallowed. His face was pale. He sat in the trail, his legs bent slightly inward, a fly buzzing around his nose.

"Easy now," he said, haltingly, shifting his gaze between the two women. "Easy, now, you two. You girls can't kill me. Neither one of you probably ever done it before. You pull that trigger, it'll haunt you till the day you die!"

Casey snapped the Winchester to her shoulder, aimed carefully, and fired. The wounded man's head snapped back so hard that Longarm thought he heard his neck crack.

"We'll see about that," Casey said tightly as the man

sagged to the ground. Cursing, she cocked a fresh cartridge into her carbine's chamber.

The two women looked around. The last man Longarm had shot groaned to Longarm's right, about twenty yards down trail. Casey and Cynthia walked back along the trail toward the man who lay on his back, belly rising and falling sharply as he breathed.

Longarm watched the two women pass below and before him, heading from his left to his right, both holding their rifles up high across their breasts. Their hair bounced on their shoulders. Their faces were set like stone.

Longarm's loins grew heavy. He gave a wry snort, and when they'd passed, he leaped from the rock to the ground and walked up trail toward the horses. When he heard the last of the four outlaws scream, he did not stop or look back. He shook his head, chuckled, and kept walking west along the trail.

Behind him, the man screamed again.

And again.

A rifle barked.

The man yelped sharply. "Oh, you fuckin' bitch! Oh! My *knee*!"

The rifle barked again.

"Oh, you've crippled me bad!" the man bellowed.

His bellowing was cut off by another rifle blast.

Then there was only silence.

Chapter 16

Late that afternoon, the sun nearly touching the tops of the western ridges, Longarm reined the sorrel to a halt and clicked back the hammer of the Winchester resting across his saddlebow.

He stared straight ahead at the old ghost town of Open Flat that was a ragged collection of log shanties and frame shacks nestled on this open stretch of high, flat desert, sandwiched between the Laramie Mountains to the south and the Snowy Range to the north. Nothing grew up this high except for bunchgrass, spindly cedars, and sage. And, apparently, tumbleweeds.

The silver-gray old ruin of a mining town was nearly buried in them.

The sky was a vast, pale blue arcing over the broad valley in which Open Flat huddled, gradually being reclaimed by the high desert prairie.

The town had boomed about ten years ago, but when the silver and copper veins pinched out, the boom went bust and the people gradually started to leave the region. Now there might have been a ranch or two in this vast area southeast of Arapaho, but the town itself was nothing but moldering timbers, broken-out windows, and disintegrating boardwalks piled high with tumbleweeds that blew here in the ceaseless wind.

Even now the wind blew, kicking up dust along the broad main street in front of Longarm, shunting miniature cyclones this way and that. A dusty shingle chain squawked, and a loose door tapped against its frame.

Besides the dust and a single tumbling tumbleweed, nothing moved. Longarm touched heels to the sorrel's flanks, and the horse clomped forward into the town, the lawman turning his head slowly from right to left and back again, appraising all the false-fronted buildings lining the street. Most had boasted paint at one time—the gaudy paint and ostentatious trim of a high-stepping mining camp—but time had long since painted them all dusty gray.

Here and there a swatch of purple or spruce green or sunrise yellow showed through the dust. But for the most part the town was colorless.

Longarm had been through the town a few times when it was booming, and a few times after the mines had played out. Last time he was here, maybe four years ago, an old fellow had been keeping a saloon open for the occasional stubborn prospector or saddle tramp with enough pocket jingle for a glass of stale ale or a venomous whiskey.

As Longarm rode ahead along the dusty street pounded to flour by thousands of ore drays, he looked around for the old watering hole, thinking there was a possibility it might still be open. But then, if he remembered right, the gent who'd run the place—he couldn't recollect the man's name nor the name of his place—had been old even then.

He'd be nearly as old as the mountains now. He'd most likely passed on. Longarm was convinced that was so when he'd reached the midway point of the three-block-long main street and hadn't spied any place that appeared to still be running.

Most of the buildings looked like the rotten teeth in a long-dead skull. And from the way things looked, if there was anyone around but the stray coyote or packrat, he'd be mighty surprised.

That was all right with Longarm. His whiskey was nearly gone, and he could use a drink, but trouble was dogging his heels in the form of the Drummond gang, and he didn't want to bring the trouble to anyone else's doorstep. He'd headed here because he'd thought it would be a good place to fort up and wait for the Drummond gang's arrival.

What was left of them, that was. He and the women had probably whittled the gang's number down to around ten or so by now. Still stiff odds, but Longarm had thrown dice against higher and lived to tell the tale.

He hipped around in his saddle and waved his rifle in the air above his head. A few seconds later, Cynthia and Casey rode out from behind a clump of rocks along the trail, a quarter mile south of town, and started riding toward him.

"Well, I'll be a pan-fried turkey buzzard," a raspy voice said out of nowhere. "If it ain't Deputy United States Marshal Custis P. Long . . ."

The unexpected voice startled Longarm as well as his

horse. The lawman held the sorrel's reins taut in his left hand while raising his rifle in his right hand.

It took his eyes a moment to pick out the old man sitting under a porch awning against one of the nondescript, age-weathered, wind-blasted buildings. Then he saw the broad, still-intact front window that was relatively clean by Open Flat standards, and the two bat-wing doors. The old man sat in a chair between them, leaning forward on a cane, a funnel-brimmed Stetson on his withered old head.

He cackled, showing maybe two, possibly three tobacco-brown teeth in his gums, and shook his head. "You didn't expect to find me still kickin', did you, Longarm?"

"Well, I'll be damned."

"You look like you're seein' a ghost!"

"Avriel . . ." Longarm said, lowering the Winchester and frowning at the old gent until his full name returned to his memory. "Avriel Simms."

"Want a drink, Longarm?"

Longarm surveyed the building behind the old man. Now that he looked more closely, he could see the badly faded sign announcing AVRIEL SIMMS OPEN FLAT SALOON in large letters that had once been green but now looked gunmetal gray behind their coating of dust and grit.

"Your place still open, Avriel?"

"Why, sure it is. You're my first customer of the day." The old man chewed on that, leaning forward on his cane and making a pensive expression. "Matter o' fact, you're my first customer of the whole week. The only one I had last week was ole Rowdy McNamara. He owns a ranch out on Bitter Creek, and when him and the old lady get to goin' at it . . ."

The oldster let his voice trail off as he turned his gaze toward Longarm's back trail. The two women were approaching now, holding their horses to slow walks, heads turned to regard the old man whose thin lips were shaping a slow, delighted smile. "Say," Simms said, "what in the name o' Sam Hill is that."

Longarm glanced behind and chuckled. "Those are called women. Surely you remember the breed, Avriel."

"Sure, sure—I remember. Don't remember ever seein' a pair as ripe as them two there, though. Holy moly!" The old man leaned forward harder, using the cane to hoist himself to his feet. He was so stoop-shouldered that even standing he appeared to be half sitting. "My, my."

"Ladies, meet Avriel Simms. He runs the saloon here in Open Flat. Avriel, meet Cynthia Larimer and Casey Summerville."

The old man shifted his weight from one old boot to another and grinned lasciviously, his washed-out blue eyes glinting copper in the severely angling sunlight. He removed his hat from his bald, age-spotted head and clamped it over his heart. "Miss Larimer, Miss Summerville, it is a privilege and an honor, and rest assured you're a sight for these sore, old eyes."

Cynthia swept a hand back through one side of her mussed hair. "I doubt that, Mr. Simms, but thank you for saying so."

"I doubt we're much of a sight for any eyes," said Casey, "but we do appreciate your saying so."

"Come on in!" Avriel said, beckoning with his hat. "Come on in and . . ."

Just then a figure appeared over the bat-wings—a woman's craggy face capped with coal-black hair that hugged her withered head like a cap. The old woman looked around, blinking, and croaked, "Who on earth are you talkin' to, you old goat?"

"Company, Gerta!" Simms said. "Come on out here and meet Longarm and his two young wimmen friends— Miss Cynthia and Miss Casey!"

The old woman seemed to flush as she stepped through the doors haltingly, brushing at her hair that was pulled tightly back and wound in a fist-sized bun behind her head. She wore what appeared a pink velvet ball gown, ratty around the edges, and a gossamer blue stole. "Well, well . . ." she said, glancing around. "Two purty girls and . . . why . . . look there . . . who'd you say the big man there is, Avriel?"

"That there is Custis P. Long—deputy U.S. marshal. Most folks call him Longarm."

"And you're welcome to, as well, Miss Gerta," Longarm said, lifting his hat straight up from his head and dipping his chin in a courtly bow.

Gerta smiled shyly, slitting her long, dark brown eyes that no doubt had been quite ravishing in their day, revealing that nowadays she had a few more teeth than Simms, but not by much. "Oh," she said. "Oh . . . how nice."

Avriel said, "This here's Gerta Breckenridge."

"Holy shit," Longarm heard himself say though he didn't think he'd said it loudly enough for anyone except him and possibly the young women to hear.

"Yessir, Gerta Breckenridge," Simms said. "Opera Queen of the New Frontier . . ."

"Sister of God with a voice like Mother Mary," Longarm finished for the man, remembering the famous line penned by a newspaper writer sometime just before the Civil War had broken out, and Gerta Breckenridge had been singing in saloons and beer tents from Texas to the northern Rockies.

"Pleased to make your acquaintance, ma'am," Longarm said, covering his chest with his hat. "Didn't know you were . . . were still in the, uh . . . profession . . ." he added, haltingly.

"Oh, I'm not in the profession anymore, Longarm. I came up here as a guest of Avriel's couple years back—I'd retired in Amarillo, don't ya know—and while I've been known to sing a few bars now an' then on Saturday night when the cowboys pull through on roundups, mostly I just keep this old mossyhorn's feet warm in his old age!"

Gerta Breckenridge glanced at the grinning Simms, tipped her head back, and cackled.

The old man wrapped an arm around her and beckoned to Longarm once more. "Go on and put your horses up in the barn behind my place. Plenty of grain an' feed. Just had some hay and parched corn shipped in from Arapaho. Then you and the ladies come on inside for some of me and Gerta's special whiskey and rattlesnake stew!"

"We don't want to intrude," Cynthia said.

"We sure don't," Longarm said, leveling a serious look at Simms. "Trouble's doggin' us. Couple hours back. The Drummond gang."

"Intrude, hell!" Gerta said before Simms could speak. "A coupla purty young gals and a tall, dark drink o' water like the one sittin' the sorrel couldn't intrude if you was bein' dogged by the devil's own yellow-fanged hounds!

Now, ya'll do as Avriel bids, and don't dally. The whiskey's still fresh, which means the rattlesnake venom hasn't settled to the bottom of the bottles yet!"

Gerta and Winters roared in ratcheting, crow-like voices as they swung around together and pushed on through the bat-wings to be consumed by the saloon's dense shadows.

Cynthia and Casey rode up to Longarm.

"What about the gang?" Cynthia asked.

"I figure we're about two hours ahead of 'em. By the time they get here, it'll be good dark. They won't try anything till morning."

"And when they do?" Casey said.

"We'll be ready for 'em." Longarm reined the sorrel around. "Come on. Let's stable these horses and accept the old folks' hospitality."

Chapter 17

As Longarm followed Cynthia and Casey through the saloon's back door and into the main drinking hall, the succulent smells of stew and fresh bread nearly laid him flat. His breath grew shallow, and an invisible fist inside him squeezed his belly. He salivated.

"Oh, my gosh," Cynthia said. They'd been riding for a couple of days now on only jerky, peaches, coffee, and water.

"What smells so good?" Casey finished for her friend.

Avriel Simms sat at a table in the middle of the long room, the bar to his left. Gerta was working at a range behind the bar and left of a large, elaborate back bar mirror lined with shelves and glasses of all shapes and sizes.

Simms said, "That's my dear Gerta's rattlesnake stew and fresh bread. That gal could sing a lick or two in her day, but these days she can cook even better!"

"Ya'll go ahead and sit down," Gerta said, cutting up a long, oval loaf of crusty brown bread. "I'll have the food over in a minute. Oh, this is just swell. Me an' Avriel haven't had a sit-down dinner with guests in a coon's age. Just a coon's age—ain't that right, honey bunch?"

"It sure is, sugar." Simms popped the cork on a whiskey bottle and winked at Longarm. "We get a little lonely out here, don't ya know. But at least we have each other." He held up the bottle. "We'll break into the whiskey later. This here's my very own special prickly pear wine. Goes right well with rattlesnake stew."

There were five bowls and five small plates on the table. Two water glasses sat before each bowl and plate, one filled with water. Avriel filled the other glasses half full with the light, safflower-colored liquid that emanated the smell of alcohol and something akin to dandelions and watermelon. Longarm and the women set their rifles on a near table.

The lawman lifted one of the glasses that Simms had poured his elixir into and sniffed.

He tasted it. He'd sampled prickly pear wine only in Texas, and he'd found it tasty enough, though no match for his rye. This stuff slid easily down his throat and spread a warm glow through his chest and shoulders. "Avriel, this is damn good. You might be onto something here—Wine of Wyoming!"

Chuckling, Simms finished pouring the prickly pear wine into the glasses. Cynthia and Casey sat down as Longarm held their chairs in turn, and then he sat down himself at the end of the table opposite the bar. From here he had a good view of the front windows on each side of the bat-wings and the street beyond.

It was almost dusk, however. Soon, he wouldn't be able to see much of anything out there.

Gerta came over and set a large, steaming pot of rattlesnake stew on the table and let everyone help themselves. Longarm thought he'd never eaten anything so delicious in his life—white chunks of rattlesnake mixed with potatoes, carrots, and peas, and all floating in a rich, pale gravy. He tore chunks of fresh bread from the loaf, and dipped the bread in the gravy, eating with his fork in one hand, bread in the other.

No one spoke during the meal. Longarm looked up a couple of times, keeping an eye on the street, and he saw both pretty women eating as hungrily as he was, shoveling the stew into their mouths and following it up with large bites of the gravy-dipped bread. Their mussed, trail-dusty hair and the color from the sun gave them a wild, desperate look that Longarm couldn't help feeling aroused by. He looked away. This was no time for his billy-goat lust.

The Drummond gang—what was left of them—could be entering town at this very moment.

After the meal, Longarm wiped his mouth with a napkin and slid his chair back from the table. "Miss Gerta, I bet that meal was tastier than the Last Supper. We do appreciate it."

The women chimed in, Cynthia reaching over and squeezing Gerta's wrinkled hand while Gerta flushed and beamed and Avriel replenished the ladies' cactus wine glasses.

"No more for me, Avriel," Longarm said, donning his hat and grabbing his Winchester off the table. "I'll be headin' out to see if it's as quiet and peaceful out there as it looks."

Cynthia slid her own chair back. "I'll join you."

"Me, too," said Casey, sipping from her refilled glass.

"You two stay and rest," Longarm said. "If I need help, you'll know soon enough. The way I figure it, when Drummond comes, we'll separate, get outside the saloon, and move around, drawing each one of them killers to us. That way, we'll have the upper hand, so to speak." Longarm winked at both women. "If they show tonight, let's just be careful not to shoot each other in the dark."

He looked at Simms. "Avriel, I do apologize for bringing trouble. When Drummond shows, you best take Gerta somewhere safe—a pantry or a root cellar, something like that."

"Don't worry—I'll take care of Gerta."

"These young ladies could use a bath and a shot of whiskey," Gerta said.

"That we could," Casey said, looking at Longarm. "But there's no time."

Longarm shook his head. "You two take that bath Gerta's offerin'. I'm headin' out to look around. If there's any trouble, you'll hear the shots. Then you'd best grab your rifles and scramble."

Longarm pinched his hat brim to the women, dug a cheroot out of his pocket, and pushed out through the saloon's bat-wing doors. He dropped down into the street, letting the darkness absorb him.

He stuck the cheroot between his teeth but did not light it. He wanted the taste of the cigar following the meal, but he'd wait and smoke it later, when he figured it was safe to show the glowing coal.

There was only a little green light left in the sky and the first stars were sparking to life. The town was dark. The breeze had died, and a silence had fallen over the broad valley in which Open Flat lay.

He glanced at the saloon's dimly lit windows behind him and then crossed the main street. At the other side, in the dense shadows of the vacant buildings, he walked back in the direction from which he and the women had ridden into the town.

The settlement stopped abruptly on the far side of a boarded-up mercantile with a broad loading dock sporting more missing floorboards than remaining ones. Here, at the base of the dock, Longarm stared off along the trail that curved across the flat—a pale tan line shrouded in the thickening darkness.

He scanned the terrain on both sides of the trail, pricking his ears. He flexed his hand around the neck of the rifle, which he held atop his right shoulder, and absently rolled the cheroot from one side of his mouth to the other.

Abruptly, he stopped rolling the cigar. He'd heard something to his right, and he turned his head to stare down along the mercantile to the rear shrouded in darkness. He wasn't sure exactly what he'd heard, but it had been something—a soft thud or a tap. Possibly someone walking around back there?

Longarm took his rifle in both hands. Slowly chambering a cartridge, he walked down along the side of the mercantile, weaving his way amongst the tumbleweeds caught up in tufts of sage and wild mahogany. He stopped at the rear corner, pressed his right shoulder against the building, and edged a look around the corner and into the dark gap behind.

He could see the weathered gray privy leaning slightly to the north and several low mounds of ancient trash that had probably been well scoured by scavengers. Beyond were several smaller buildings—sheds of a sort.

As he stared between two such structures, he saw a shadow move so quickly that he instantly wondered if it was merely the breeze jostling a branch and thus moving a shadow. But no. There was no breeze. The night was as still and quiet as an amphitheater, with shadows growing now as the moon began its rise above the southeastern mountains, spreading a faint sphere of lilac around it.

Longarm squeezed the rifle in his hands and, clamping down on the cigar in his teeth, stepped out into the mercantile's backyard. Looking around carefully, walking on the balls of his boots, he strode past the privy and covered the twenty-yard gap between the privy and a corral against which many tumbleweeds had blown, forming a shaggy wall. There was a stable on the corral's far side, with a small log cabin hunched to the stable's left, with about a twenty-foot gap between the two buildings.

Longarm had seen the shadow move somewhere in there . . .

He proceeded slowly forward, peering into the corral and then into the gap ahead of him. Once inside the gap between buildings, he pressed his back against the stable and cast his gaze at the cabin.

It was a long, brush-roofed affair with a stone chimney on the far side. It appeared long abandoned, brush growing up along the foundations. The two windows facing Longarm—one on each side of the door—had been broken out. Something told Longarm to investigate it. But he'd taken only two steps before he heard a soft thump from inside the stable behind him.

He whipped around. The moon had climbed high enough that it shed some milky light over the stable, revealing that the plank board door stood about two feet open. Longarm glanced once more at the cabin and then moved toward the stable, lowering the barrel of his Winchester and extending the gun straight out from his right hip.

He nudged the door open with the barrel of his rifle, stepped quickly inside, tightening his finger on the trigger. Two small lights flickered before him, from about ten feet away. A shrill snarl rose, and Longarm drew back on the Winchester's trigger just before he eased the tension, knowing in the back of his mind what he was confronting just before the lights—or eyes, rather—disappeared.

The cat's head—he recognized the pointed, tufted ears of a bobcat—moved in front of a window on the other side of the stable. Then the head disappeared as the cat with its bobbed tail soundlessly leaped out the broken-out window to the ground.

Longarm heaved a sigh and lowered the rifle. At the same time, he told himself, "Wait—something scared the cat in here." The admonition had no sooner passed through his mind than he threw himself back against the wall beside the open door as a rifle flashed and cracked behind him.

The report drummed raucously in the gap between the buildings. The slug careened through the open door to slam into the stable's opposite wall. Longarm twisted around the door frame, poking his rifle outside.

A man-shaped silhouette stood in the open door of the cabin on the other side of the gap. Longarm fired the Winchester twice, both spent cartridges arcing over his right shoulder to clink together on the stable floor.

The bushwhacker gave a chuff and flew back into the cabin, hitting the cabin's floor with a crunching thud and rattle of spurs.

He'd just slammed a fresh round into the action when something cold, hard, and round pressed against the side of his head, just beneath his hat. A low, resonant voice said, "Drop the Winchester."

Longarm froze. He slid his eyes to the right and could see the shadow of the man holding the gun. He could hear the man breathing, smell the sweat-and-leather perfume wafting off of him.

"One more time," the man said, dipping his voice in warning, "drop the Winchester."

Longarm depressed the rifle's hammer and tossed the gun onto the ground. The man holding the gun against his head reached around Longarm's belly, released the keeper thong over Longarm's Colt, and slipped the piece from the holster. He wedged it behind his own cartridge belt.

He pressed Longarm's head sideways with the barrel of his own gun. "Now, let's go see what's cookin' over at Ole Simms's saloon. All right? Sound good to you, cowboy? I'm bettin' there's some scrumptious female flesh we should see about."

Longarm turned his head to rake his eyes across the man—a little shorter than Longarm and wearing a black hat, a green neckerchief, and a self-satisfied grin—as Longarm turned and started walking forward along the gap, in the direction of the main street and the saloon.

Chapter 18

As Longarm walked through the gap between the large mercantile building and another, smaller structure beside it, he thought about the double-barreled derringer snuggling inside his vest pocket, opposite his watch. His right hand twitched. He brushed it against his hip as he continued walking, glancing back at the man behind him.

Bright moonlight glinted off the barrel of the Remington the man was aiming at him.

The man rammed the gun against Longarm's back, shoving him forward. "What the hell you lookin' at? You just keep movin', mister. We'll see what Colt has in store for you. Whatever it is, after all our boys you killed, it ain't gonna be good."

"They were tryin' to kill me," Longarm said with a caustic chuff.

"You just hold your tongue an' keep walkin'."

At the head of the gap between the two buildings,

Longarm turned and began walking toward the saloon. He could see the dimly lit windows. A half dozen or so horses were tied to the hitch racks out front of the place. The closer he got to the Open Flat, the more shadows he could see moving around in front of the windows.

He thought about the women, and his gut clenched.

He envisioned the derringer residing in his vest pocket. His hand twitched. He brushed it across his hip again, and sweat broke out atop his upper lip, dampening his mustache.

His heart was beating faster. He had to do something before he got to the saloon, but getting himself killed wasn't going to help anything. The gent behind him had the Remington centered on his back. Longarm doubted that he could get anywhere close to sliding the derringer from his vest pocket, clicking back one of the two hammers, and getting himself turned around to aim the piece at the man behind him before a bullet flung from the Remington shattered his spine.

He had to wait for an opportunity.

Meanwhile, he reached the saloon and the horses standing wearily at the hitch rack—a couple of pintos, a couple of duns, a piebald, a paint . . .

He glanced over the horses only absently. The hot, dusty beasts seemed ominous, standing there in front of the saloon, which could very well be the end of his as well as Cynthia and Casey's trail. Moonlight glinted on the saddles and in the eyes of one of the horses looking curiously back at Longarm.

The lawman walked up the porch steps.

He glanced once more over over his shoulder. The

man behind was keeping a few paces back—too far away
for Longarm to try to swing on him before he'd almost
certainly get a bullet in his guts.

Longarm crossed the dilapidated porch and stopped
in front of the bat-wings, looking over the doors and
inside the saloon lit by several candles and two lamps.
There were six or seven men in the place, and they were
all sitting or standing around the tables about halfway
between the front and the back.

Avriel Simms sat in a chair. Two of the outlaws stood
around him and another sat in a chair facing him while
leaning one elbow on a table flanking him. One of the
men stood crouching over the old man, threat in the set
of his shoulders. Just now that man slapped Simms with
the back of his hand, whipping his arm fiercely. Longarm
winced at the sharp crack and Simms's groan. Longarm
bulled through the bat-wings, teeth gritted.

"Leave the old man alone, you chicken-livered son of
a bitch!"

The man behind Longarm slammed the barrel of the
Remington against the back of Longarm's head. It was
a glancing blow, but it still evoked a tolling of bells in
the lawman's head and caused his legs to buckle. His
knees hit the floor with a thundering boom. All the outlaws in the room swung toward him, whipping hoglegs
from holsters or reaching for rifles.

The outlaw sitting in front of old Simms turned his
head toward Longarm. The lawman hadn't gotten a clear
view of Drummond the other night, but this man had to
be him. His face was wet and pale, and his lips were
stretched back from his teeth in a living death grimace.
The whites of his eyes were yellow beneath the brim of

his funnel-brimmed black hat with a hammered silver
band.

"Who the fuck . . . ?" Drummond let his voice trail
off as he turned the death grimace into a smile of sorts.
He winced as he gained his feet and turned his stocky
frame toward Longarm. His lower right side was bright
with fresh blood. The stain extended halfway down the
thigh of his right leg and across the front of his belly.
There was another, drier stain higher up on the other side.
That's where Longarm had shot him, but the lawman saw
now that his own bullet must have only burned the killer.
It was Casey's slug that was grieving him—likely going
to kill him soon.

Drummond stood stoop-shouldered, haggard, pain-
racked—like a wounded bull elk who'd found himself
cornered in a box canyon.

"Longarm," he said. "Shoulda known."

Longarm frowned up at the man. He couldn't remember having run into the renegade before.

"Sure, I know you," Drummond said. "You may not
know me, but I know you. Big, brown-haired, brown-
eyed hombre with a face like a mean, old bull buff, and
a longhorn mustache. Hell, most of my kind's either seen
or heard about the famous Custis P. Long—deputy U.S.
marshal!"

He said this last with extra venom, spitting the words
out like sour grapes, so that the others could hear. They
all looked with keen interest at the big man kneeling on
the floor before them, canting their heads this way and
that, grinning.

"Longarm—no shit, Colt?" asked a tall man with

long, curly gray hair and black brows and mustache. He looked skeptically at Drummond.

"No shit, Frank—that there is the Long Arm of the Law his own self. Should have known it was him followin' us. Who else could cut down as many men as he did, steal into our camp, shootin' me in the gut and leavin' me to die *slow*!"

He shouted that last, jerking his head up and down like a rabid cur.

Longarm smiled woodenly. "Oh, but if you remember," he said jeeringly, "it was the girl's bullets that—"

"Shut up, you fuckin' liar!" Drummond was the only one in the room not holding a gun. He staggered toward Longarm, clenching his fists at his sides.

Obviously, he hadn't told his men that Casey had shot him with his own gun. That would have made him look foolish. Instead, he told them he was surprised by the big man stealing into their camp while he'd been giving the girl a good time, and then dragged her away.

"I'll deal with you later, Longarm. In my own creative way. Like maybe bury you neck-deep in the street so's me and the boys can take target practice on your ears."

"Jesus," Longarm said, rubbing the back of his head, "that would hurt like hell."

Just then two men appeared atop the stairs, each coming from a different direction and then dropping down the staircase. Each held a rifle. Drummond looked up at them. "Any sign of the girl?"

The first one coming down the stairs shook his head. "There's two tubs filled with hot water in a room up there, but no girl."

Longarm slid his gaze from the two newcomers to Drummond, who turned to Longarm, frowning. "Who's your third rider, Longarm?" He smiled lasciviously through his tobacco-stained teeth. "Not another girl, is it?"

Longarm shrugged as he gained his feet heavily. "Wouldn't you like to know?"

Drummond glanced at the two men who'd just descended the stairs. "Boys, tie this famous *lawman* to a chair. If we can't get where the girl . . . or *girls* . . . are out of the old man, we'll start on him. Leastways, I wanna know where he is, 'cause later he's gonna do some howlin'."

The two men headed for Longarm, swinging wide to get around him. He had no intention of being tied to a chair. That just meant he'd be dead soon, and there'd be nothing he could do about it. He aimed to move while he still could, even if it meant dying here and now.

At least he'd take some of these sons o' bitches with him.

Longarm sighed and feigned an expression of defeat as the two men approached from the stairs. When the first was three feet away, Longarm shoved his right hand into his vest pocket, and plucked out the derringer. He quickly thumbed back both triggers and sent one round careening through the left eye of the man nearest him and the second round through the forehead of the man behind the first.

He dropped the derringer, which dangled by its gold-washed chain from his old railroad turnip residing in the opposite vest pocket, and was reaching for the rifle of the first man he'd just killed when the man behind him slammed his pistol across Longarm's head for a second time.

Longarm staggered forward, holding his head in his arms, fireworks flashing behind his squeezed-shut eyes, and felt the floor come up to slam him hard about the chest and shoulders. He heard himself groan against the throbbing pain in his head.

"Oh, for cryin' out loud!" Drummond shouted, filling both his hands with the two long-barreled revolvers he wore in holsters on his thighs. "I was going to give you some time, Longarm, but I see you just can't behave. Gonna have to put you down like the rabid cur you are!"

Longarm looked up. Drummond stood before him, about five feet away, extending both pistols straight out before him, angled down. "Let it be known from this day forward that Custis P. Long, known by friend and foe as Longarm, was killed this day by none other than Colt Drummond, his own mean an' nasty self!"

Something squawked near Longarm. He glanced to his right to see a two-by-two-foot door open in the faded-green, wainscoted front of the bar, about six inches above the floor. Gerta Breckenridge's prune-like, brown-eyed face peered through the door.

The old woman hardened her jaws as she poked a double-barreled shotgun out the dark opening, and squinted her eyes as she snarled, "Take this you limp-dicked, woman-rapin', tinhorn bastard!"

Longarm dropped his head to the floor as the old woman extended the shotgun over his prone body, and . . .

Ka-boommmm!

The entire room jumped as the first barrel's hammer slammed down on a wad of double-ought buck. Longarm turned his head to see Colt Drummond hurled up and back, screaming and triggering both pistols into the ceiling. As he fell onto a table, breaking it in two pieces and tumbling to the floor, Gerta cut loose with the shotgun's second barrel.

It was like a giant slamming his fist on the room.

The man who'd hazed Longarm into the saloon went flying back out the bat-wings, across the porch, and into the street.

Longarm saw a rifle lying on the floor five feet away. He probably wouldn't reach it before the others started cutting loose, but he shook off the searing pain in the back of his head, bolted off his heels, leaped for the rifle, and grabbed it in both hands. He rolled over, quickly jacking a round into the chamber, and extended the gun toward the rest of the gang, all of whom were now yelling and leaping into action, bearing down on both Longarm and Gerta.

Longarm thought he might be able to get one before they sent him on over the divide, and he did, drilling the man in his right cheek, just above his shaggy patch beard and where a knife scar made a teardrop pattern. Then the rifles really started bellowing and Longarm squeezed his eyes closed, waiting for the lead shower that was sure to shred the skin from his bones, leaving nothing more than a pile of blood puddling on the floor where he now lie.

His hands kept working as though of their own accord and he was surprised as hell to find that he was able to aim the rifle from the floor once more and cut loose on the shooters. Only, there wasn't much use.

They were stumbling and flying and twisting around like a bunch of drunk Irish muleskinners at a Rocky

Mountain hoedown. It was as though the floor were pitching around, knocking the killers from left to right and from front to back, and back again.

They were not the ones shooting.

Cynthia had bounded through the bat-wings and firing from a crouch while Casey must have entered the saloon through the back door. She was cutting loose with her own Winchester, aiming quickly, triggering, ejecting the spent cartridge, aiming again, and firing.

Longarm stared in amazement at the two women and the billowing cloud of power smoke before him. To his right, Gerta Breckenridge was cackling like a witch and yelling, "You go, ladies—shoot them killers down dead! Oh, this is too good for them! Oh, have it, ladies! Now, that's some fine old-fashioned shootin' if I ever seen it!"

Longarm glanced toward where Avriel Simms had been sitting in his chair. Now the old man lay flat on the floor near the overturned chair, arms clamped over his head, wriggling around as though he were trying to squirm down between the floorboards.

The cacophony lasted for only about fifteen seconds.

Then the hammer of Cynthia's Winchester landed on an empty chamber. A second later, Casey's did, as well.

A silence fell over the room.

Longarm blinked as he stared over his own aimed rifle at the smoky room. The outlaws lay in bloody, bullet-torn piles on the floor and across tables and overturned chairs. One man sighed and rolled from his shoulder to his belly, shook, and lay still.

And that was the end of them.

"Like I said—that's some shootin'," Gerta said, crawling out the trapdoor in the bar—which had probably been used for stocking the shelves beneath the bar when the saloon was booming with the rest of Open Flat.

She cackled and extended a hand to Longarm. "Wasn't it, Marshal Long? Say, you don't look so good."

Longarm had pushed off a knee and was halfway to both feet, but the room was spinning like a top.

"Say, there, Marshal," came Avriel Simms's voice from a thousand miles away. "Gerta's right. Why, you'd best . . ."

Longarm didn't hear the rest. Darkness overtook him. And then he was vaguely aware of scrambling footsteps and being eased to the floor before he was aware of nothing at all for about three seconds—or what seemed like three seconds—until he opened his eyes to see a bare breast with a perfect pink nipple jostling around in front of his face. He stared at the nipple, blinking, incredulous.

He must be dreaming.

But then he felt several hands caressing him with damp cloths and he turned to see another pair of breasts jostling at his side opposite the first pair. He looked up to see Cynthia smiling down at him.

"I think he's coming around," she said. She lowered her head, kissed his lips. "Easy, sweetheart. You just lay still and let Casey and I tend to you."

He was as naked as the day he was born.

He lay in a bed with a charcoal brazier glowing nearby. He must be upstairs in the saloon. Two candles guttered on a dresser, shunting shadows this way and that. They slid gold-limned silhouettes across the young women's naked bodies—still warm and damp from a recent bath.

"I'll say he's coming around," Casey said.

Cynthia laughed.

Longarm looked down past his belly and saw that his cock was at half-mast and growing.

Casey touched the tip of her finger to the swollen head and arched a brow at Cynthia. "Do you mind?"

"Dear," said Cynthia, "what better way to help you over this horrible tragedy. Besides, he's way too good for me not to share him."

The hellcats giggled and bounced around on their knees, making the bed shake. Casey glanced at Longarm, shook her long, blond hair back behind her shoulders, and lowered her head to his crotch.

"Mmmm," she said, sucking and licking. "So good . . ."

Soon the head of his cock was causing her cheek to bulge.

Longarm ground his heels into the bed and groaned.

Watch for

LONGARM AND THE LYING LADIES

the 420ᵀᴴ novel in the exciting Longarm
series from Jove

Coming in November!